Cynthia Starts a Band

CYNTHIA STARTS A BAND

A Novel

OLIVIA SWINDLER

NEW YORK

LONDON • NASHVILLE • MELBOURNE • VANCOUVER

Cynthia Starts a Band
A Novel

Published in New York, New York, by Morgan James Publishing. Morgan James is a trademark of Morgan James, LLC. www.MorganJamesPublishing.com

Morgan James BOGO™

A **FREE** ebook edition is available for you or a friend with the purchase of this print book.

CLEARLY SIGN YOUR NAME ABOVE

Instructions to claim your free ebook edition:
1. Visit MorganJamesBOGO.com
2. Sign your name CLEARLY in the space above
3. Complete the form and submit a photo of this entire page
4. You or your friend can download the ebook to your preferred device

ISBN 9781631954900 paperback
ISBN 9781631954917 ebook
Library of Congress Control Number:
2021931233

Cover Design by:
Megan Dillon
megan@creativeninjadesigns.com

Interior Design by:
Chris Treccani
www.3dogcreative.net

Morgan James PUBLISHING Builds with... Habitat for Humanity® Peninsula and Greater Williamsburg

Morgan James is a proud partner of Habitat for Humanity Peninsula and Greater Williamsburg. Partners in building since 2006.

Get involved today! Visit
MorganJamesPublishing.com/giving-back

To those who carried me when I started over.

Acknowledgments

I am forever grateful to my sister, Grace, who has spent countless hours listening to my thousand different story ideas. She not only makes me a better writer but challenges me to be a better person. She is my best friend, favorite person to laugh with, and is the only person to read everything I have written (some very crappy songs included . . .) The next few bottles of wine are on me.

I am so grateful to my dad, who not only encouraged my dream of being a writer but taught me how to love and treat people with dignity and respect. He instilled in me the desire to learn how to say things "in other words." This concept has challenged me as a writer and storyteller. I love you. I promise someday I'll write a story about finding Jim.

This book would not be readable if it was not for my incredible editor, Elizabeth J. Gabriele. Thank you for the countless hours of work (and voice notes) put into making this book beautiful! Thank you for your intentionality and ability to make a story come to life. I am so grateful for your skills as an editor, but more than anything, I am thankful for your friendship.

Thank you to my team at Morgan James for believing in this book. It has been such an honor to be welcomed with open arms into your publishing family. Thank you to Karen Anderson who met with me when I had no idea what to do next. Thank you to Terri Riehl, who connected me with Karen and Morgan James.

Writing a book was a beautiful reminder that I truly have the best community. My roommate, Gwen, not only listened to me talk for hours about this book but was the first person to read it. Her encouragement was priceless, and she helped me to believe that I could actually publish a book. She also spent many hours explaining the proper usage of a comma. This book could not have happened without her. Thank you to Ashley and Blake for keeping me smiling during the season when this book was written. You spread joy like confetti and are the most talented musicians I have ever met in real life. Ashley was also one of this book's first readers. I am deeply thankful for your willingness and grace with my many spelling blunders. You are a true friend.

For years and years my dear friend, Mary, and I have talked about the books we were drafting. I am so thankful for not only years of friendship, but her support in all that I have dreamed to create. Thank you for being my person, through thick and thin. Billy, I love you.

I am so grateful for my friends who volunteered to read the earliest versions of this book. It is such a privilege to have friends who will endure spelling errors and plot holes. In addition to those already mentioned, I would like to specifically thank Molly, Grace, Ellen, Amy, Beth, Casey, Katie, and Alyssa. I love each of you so much.

I would not be the person I am today if it was not for the support of my family. I feel so grateful for the way all my aunts and uncles have loved and mentored me through the years. Thank you to my Aunt Linda for being one of the first readers of this book. Your support has helped me be the person I am today. I am sorry

I didn't make this a murder mystery. Also incredibly formative in who I am are my aunts Pix and Kim. You both make me laugh until I cry and remind me how to be a good friend. Thank you for wanting to read this book and always encouraging me in my writing. Like Eleanor, I also grew up with cousins who would move mountains for me. So many of my favorite memories are filled with cousins, in Chelan or on Suzy's porch. I love you all. Kristy's relationship with Eleanor was inspired by my friendship with my cousins, Chloe and Paige.

I moved to France in 2016, lonely and weary. I would not have made it through that year without Amy, Ruth, Amanda, and Esther. If it had not been for our Tuesday night shenanigans, this book would not have been possible. 2016 was also made brighter by Roommate Grace, Molly, Casey, Ellen, Paige, Alyssa, Meghan, Sarah, Bayley, and Sydney. Thank you for answering the phone even when you knew you would be met with tears on the other end. I have since developed a small family here in France. *Je vous aime.*

And finally, I write in memory of my mother. I will babs talk until the day I die. Everything I know about telling a good story I inherited from her. She grew up in rural western Pennsylvania; Eleanor's band is named in her honor.

Prologue

I guess I always thought disappearing—starting over—would be easy. People did it in movies all the time, right? Got new passports, changed their names, bought bus tickets heading to some nowhere/no-name town. Or, if they were really escaping, they bought two or three tickets to throw everyone off their trail. They never told anyone where they were going; maybe someday they would send a cryptic letter to let their friends or family know they are okay.

And then, freedom. Getting to start over. To see the world with new eyes. Sure, you might never hug your loved ones again; but it might be worth it, depending on what—or who—you were escaping.

I had thought it was going to be easy—that I would be able to slip from the limelight and into the life of an unknown person. I just wanted to go to the grocery store without being assaulted by flashing lights and cameras. I wanted to be able to walk into a room and not feel eyes critiquing my every move. I wanted someone to ask me where I was from because they genuinely had no idea who I was.

I would slip into oblivion. I would be a person unknown. I would get to start over.

That was my only option, after all.

August 24th

Cynthia

I had no idea what day of the week it was, but that was normal for me. Days of the week meant nothing to me when we were touring. My internal calendar instead went like this: today, the bus will take us there, and then tomorrow, we will get back on the bus and be there. It didn't matter if it was Tuesday or Friday; all days had the same value.

On the other hand, this was the first time in a long time I hadn't needed to incessantly check the clock on my phone. I wasn't afraid of being late to a soundcheck. I didn't feel that familiar pit in my stomach telling me that I had overslept and would be late for hair and makeup.

For the first time in years, my time was mine.

I opened my eyes and peered out the window. We were cruising along a major highway. I was sure that I had been on this road at some point in my life before. Before, this road had meant nothing, but now the same open road meant freedom.

I had told the ticket salesman that I wanted a ticket to get to Seattle—although I had no real idea of how to get there. I wasn't even sure if I knew precisely where Seattle was. I had visited Seattle plenty of times, but it had been clouded by the tour haze. I knew it was a big city, which meant I would be able to slip into my new life there without standing out.

I hadn't realized how far away Seattle was from Denver. They were both on the West Coast; somehow, I had figured it would only take a few hours to get from one to the other. They had always been so close together on our schedule.

In Portland, I changed buses. The stop made me surer than ever of my decision.

I had done it. I had gotten out.

It still didn't feel real. I had dreamed about this moment for so long, without ever actually believing it would happen.

I hadn't told anyone that I was leaving, but I was sure they knew by now.

After the incident, I had walked out of the arena and gone straight to the bus station. I hadn't even bothered getting my things from my bus or the dressing room. It hadn't occurred to me that I should have withdrawn some cash. I would get some money soon. If they wanted to find me, they would check my credit card statements. I had seen enough action movies to know this was usually the first thing checked when looking for a missing person: a credit card trail.

I guessed I also needed to change my name. Or at least go by a different one? I really hadn't thought this part of the plan through very well.

When we were first starting out, someone had asked me if I planned on using a stage name. "Everyone does it," I was told. But I was sixteen at the time and thought there was something cool about seeing my name up in lights. That was me! My real name. At no point had I imagined that I would need a pseudonym.

If I had gone by a stage name, this might have been easier. I could have just reverted to who I had been before the world cared about who I had become.

I needed the opposite of a stage name.

I reached for my phone—at least I had had the presence of mind to grab that—and had another realization: I would probably have to get a new phone. After checking the runaway's credit card activity, people always tracked their phones. There was something techy that could be done by pinging off cell towers. I wasn't sure what that meant, but I had seen it in enough movies to be wary of calling anyone.

I looked down at my lit-up phone screen.

Of course, he had called. It would have been stupid to expect otherwise.

I didn't have to call him back. A weight lifted from my shoulders, and I took a deep, shuddering breath. I was free! I never had to call him back ever again.

James had called me twenty-three times, to be exact. While I had expected that, I still felt a slight pang of remorse. I had known James since high school. I was just a long-legged teenager when he became our manager. We had walked through everything together. He had turned me from a gangly teenage girl to a polished pop star. And here I was, on a bus, running away.

I needed to let James know I was safe. I felt like I owed him at least that.

I turned off all the location services on my phone. I didn't know if that would actually do anything, but at least I felt a little more secure.

"I am safe. Promise. Will call if I can." I texted. But I knew that I was never going to call.

I needed a plan.

While I had been fantasizing about this escape for months, it had always felt like something belonging to the distant future, like a dream that would never come to fruition. Now, it was actually happening, and I needed to figure out my next move.

One of my cousins, Kristy, lived in Seattle. I needed to let her know I was coming. She and I had always been close. If I could stay with her, I wouldn't have to put something else on my credit card. Maybe she could front me the money for a hotel. I had never had to do any of this by myself before. I wasn't sure if I even knew how to get a hotel room. Or how to figure out which hotel was decent and safe. These things had always been taken care of for me.

In fact, now that I thought about it, this was the first time that I was able to choose for myself. No one was telling me what I needed to wear. No one was telling me what time I needed to go to bed or wake up. No one had made a dinner reservation for me in Seattle. I didn't have any obligation to make an appearance. For the first time in as long as I could remember, I had the freedom to make my own decisions.

The entire bus ride had been filled with peace and quiet. It was almost too much to take in all at once.

The only decision I had made for myself in the recent past was my decision to leave. I could not have imagined how many subsequent decisions would result.

I could feel myself getting overwhelmed. Was this really what I desired? The events of the previous hours flashed through my mind. I wanted to hide. I had abandoned my life without a second thought or a clear plan of what to do next.

What had I done? I had left the life that most people only dreamed of living, and for what? Nothing? I had no plan. No boyfriend. I had given no warning to my friends or family. There was no promise of another job (though it wasn't like I would need the money). But I was starting to realize that this was probably not my most responsible decision.

James had once told me that I was his favorite client because I always did what I was told. He never had to worry about me getting caught in the wrong bar or getting cited with a DUI. I was a dream client. I did what I was told, and people loved me.

Maybe they just loved the person James had made me into. I wasn't sure that person had ever been me.

James had texted me back right away, "Ellie, you need to call me right now. Your bus had to leave without you. The plane is already waiting for you in Denver. Go to the airport now, and you will be able to meet us in Dallas by soundcheck."

I was not going to get on that plane. I was not going to make it in time for soundcheck. A piece of my soul had been slowly suffocating. I knew my choice was not just affecting me; this was James's life as well. The lives of the rest of the band. But after last night, I knew I wouldn't be able to continue as Eleanor Quinn.

They could do the set without me. Our publicist would release some statement about how I had come down with bronchitis or lupus. It would be something nasty (but not life-threatening), and I would rejoin the tour as soon as I was cleared.

The publicist would be lying.

I would not be rejoining the tour. After what happened, I couldn't be Eleanor Quinn, singer extraordinaire from Kittanning. I was going to become someone new.

Outside the window, the road markers flashed past, dimmed by the rain. The bus passed a billboard advertising a weight loss company that had helped a woman named Cynthia lose seventy-five pounds. I was going to be Cynthia. Cynthia, who had just lost more than seventy-five figurative pounds of a band that had been controlling her every waking moment.

I ignored James's text. I didn't know how to tell him that I would not be on the plane. It felt unfair to him. I had never intended for him to end up in the crosshairs of my consequences. Our lives had become intertwined; that was just the harsh reality. But I couldn't let that change my mind. I would figure out how to break the news to him once I had settled. The tour was going to take a week off after Dallas, so that would give them time to regroup.

I tried to focus on that.

Giving up on my vain attempt to shove my guilt aside, I started searching for Kristy's number. It was almost 8:00 a.m. This, I thought to myself, was when most people got up. I checked my phone and saw that it was a Tuesday. She worked for Amazon, and the last time I'd seen her, she had mentioned how long and crazy the hours were, so it was a safe assumption that she would be either getting ready or on her way to work. Or maybe already there.

Her phone started ringing.

"Hey, El, what's up! Why are you calling so early? Didn't you have a show last night?"

Okay, so she hadn't heard about the incident.

"It's a long story, and I can't tell you over the phone." I was still worried about those nasty cell tower pings, "Basically, I'm on a Grayhen heading to Seattle. Can I stay with you?"

"Wait, what? You mean a . . . Greyhound? Uh . . . yes, of course, what time does your bus get in? I'll pick you up."

"Oh, yeah, a Greyhound, and I can't tell you more over the phone. I think we should be there in, like, two hours. Is that okay?"

"Yes, I'll be there."

"Hey, also, could you bring me a change of clothes?"

Kristy was waiting for me on the bus platform, clearly dressed for work, brown hair twisted into an easy, elegant bun. I was impressed. I realized that if I had gotten a call like that, I wouldn't have even known where the bus stop was, let alone on which platform to wait.

As soon as I stepped off the bus, she burst out laughing.

"What on earth are you wearing?"

"This is why I asked for a change of clothes," I motioned down to my cobalt-blue bejeweled onesie. "Isn't this what the kids are wearing in Seattle? This is all the rage in New York right now." I tried to joke.

She looked over the top of her designer glasses at me: "You know, they probably are. I've never really been able to keep up with what kids are wearing these days."

Kristy was eight months older than me. When we were kids, that eight-month gap had felt like years. It meant that she was a grade above me in school. She got her license before me. She experienced everything just a bit before me.

If only we had known as kids that our lives would turn out so differently.

She walked me over to her car. On the passenger seat sat a bottle of wine, a change of clothes, and a bar of chocolate. I knew what this meant.

"Is there a video? Oh gosh. How bad is it?"

"Well, it's not all bad. You guys went viral, which is something most people only dream of!"

"Kristy, my whole life has been viral for like the past year."

"Okay, fair point."

We drove in silence for a few blocks. The weight of the unspoken was almost unbearable.

"So," Kristy broke the silence first, "Do you want to talk about it?"

I thought about this for a second. The request was expected. After all, I had just barged into my cousin's life without any warning. The familiar fear of letting someone down wormed its way into my heart.

I barely managed: "I don't think I know how to yet." It was the only honest answer I could give. The incident flashed through my mind. Again.

Kristy smiled warmly from the driver's seat, "That's okay." And, just like that, the weight on my chest lifted just a little more.

January 2nd

Eleanor

When Eleanor was a kid, maybe six or seven, she could often be found with a hairbrush in her hand, singing songs she had written that had meaning to only her. Even then, she had known she loved more than just music. The people, the cheering, the crowds, the bass, and the lights were all so much more than beautiful words.

Fast forward to Monday, three months before her next tour was scheduled to begin, and everything in her missed the rush of performing.

Some artists don't like to perform. They love being in the studio, writing, and recording. Not Eleanor. If she had it her way, she would never step into a studio again. There was something terrible about the vulnerability of watching the words she had spent hours writing being slashed and moved and erased. There was nothing enjoyable about spending hours debating over a single line or instrument or key change.

Sure, that stuff was crucial. But Eleanor was made for the stage. For the rush of adrenaline right before a show. The feeling of a crowd yelling for you, the joy that came with stepping out in front of them. It was like an amplified show and tell. Come world, see this thing I have created, celebrate with me the way it makes us both feel.

I only have to wait three more months. Anyone can wait for three months, she thought to herself.

It was the first sunny day the city had seen in a long time. She kept an apartment in New York more out of necessity than a desire to live in the city. The band quickly learned to stay close to each other and the studio when writing and recording. If she had her way, she would spend her time off the road on her family's farm outside of Pittsburgh. However, she needed to be able to get to the studio at a moment's notice, so she begrudgingly put up with living in the city.

There had been something blissful about growing up on the farm. Most of Eleanor's childhood memories involved running barefoot, bleached blonde, and sunburnt through her grandfather's cow pasture to her grandparents' house. Six days out of seven, her aunts would be gathered in the kitchen, cooking and gossiping. They were just the right kind of aunts: comfortable in every way. It was the perfect place to grow up. She would sneak onto the front porch and listen to them chat as she pretended to read a book and imagined what her life would look like when she was their age.

Grabbing a book, she headed out into the sunshine, the morning rays warming her face. She was a morning person. This was a hard reality on the road; it wasn't easy being a morning person when your job forced you to stay out late. So, when she found herself at home, these were some of her favorite moments.

She was only allowed twenty minutes of peace before her phone started to ring.

It was James. From Eleanor's perspective, James had a way of calling at the most inopportune moments. Maybe this was a reflex that came when you had known someone most of your life and spent almost every day together. A certain rhythm developed after spending that much time in the same room—a finely honed instinct for the most bothersome time to call the other.

"Hi, James," she answered, using her best you-are-bothering-me voice.

"Hey, Ellie!" he started, ignoring the tone, "Listen, I need to talk to you about a song."

The band was in the final weeks before the album's release. To Eleanor, everything should have been good to go. She had spent countless nights on the phone, in the studio, making last-minute changes. The band had agreed that the album was ready. The first single had dropped on Friday, and it was already one of the most streamed songs of the weekend. Everyone—James included—was feeling pretty good about the album, which was why Eleanor could not think of a reason why he would be calling.

"Yes, James."

"I need you to write a love song." It came off like a question . . . as if he already knew what her reaction was going to be.

"James, this isn't for Kittanning's brand-new album, is it?"

He was silent.

"James."

"Listen, the label had one more listen-through, and we decided you need to add a love song. The world needs a love song."

"James, I wrote love songs. The album is full of love songs. I don't want to write a fluffy filler song just because you suddenly don't think the album is complete."

"They don't want another fluff song." She noticed that he went from "we" to "they." At the end of the day, James was always on her side. He would side with her before he would with the label.

"What do they want, James."

"They want you to write a duet. The label wants you and Art to sing a duet together."

"You know that there is no way that he is going to go for that." She tried to suppress a laugh.

"Well, then you better write something he can't resist singing."

"James, you can't make me do this. First, he never wants to sing what I write. Never mind that I wrote our entire last album! Second, he is not a sappy-song singer. He is not going to go for some gushy love ballad, especially one that he has to sing with me."

"Let me deal with Art. But let me just tell you that this is not an 'if you feel like it' ask."

"Fine, let me see what I can come up with."

She hung up the phone with a huff.

She did not want to be the girl who only writes love songs. And, most of all, she did not want to be the girl that had to sing a duet with Art. They wasted enough energy already attempting to convince the world they were best friends. They had been doing this for years, and, up until now, they had escaped singing a duet. There was nothing she wanted to do less than write the stupid song.

Her phone beeped again: a text from James.

Thankful for you!

What a suck-up.

Moments later, another message arrived, this time from Art.

Are you kidding me?! Whatever. Just don't write a bomb.

She didn't respond to either message.

It wasn't that Art and Eleanor were enemies, but they did not get along. Had it not been for Kittanning, they would have continued with their lives, happily ignoring the existence of the other. When they were not touring or interviewing, they did not talk. According to Eleanor's mother, this was because Eleanor had too large of an ego. She thought it was outrageous to believe that Art was a jerk.

"How could someone with cheekbones like his be a jerk?" was her mother's most recent quote. It's true that Art was tall and dark, charming with his soulful eyes and a chiseled jaw. He was the kind of guy that made you look twice.

Eleanor stared at the piece of paper in front of her. She had been writing songs since she knew what music was. People who didn't write music think it just 'flows out,' like an extension of her personality. Cute and easy, right?

Sometimes it was like that. Sometimes, the song wrote itself. It was like giving birth; it had to come out of her, and she wouldn't be able to eat or sleep until she had given it life.

Other times, it was staring at a blank sheet of paper. For hours.

There was nothing there, and there might never be. It was like the yips. You did something all your life, and then one day, you couldn't. This was especially true under pressure. The label needed something beautiful and chart-worthy, and they needed it now.

There was nothing in her that felt inspired to create, except her need to make James happy.

She tried to think about the last time she had been in love. She needed to channel some of that energy. Maybe the memory of someone would help.

She couldn't remember the last time she had been on a date. Dating was more problematic than one might imagine in her line of work. She couldn't just go out for a drink undetected. Also, going back to step one, how did you even meet someone? Was this future potential someone actually interested in Eleanor or interested in her career and clout? She still believed there was a difference between Eleanor Quinn, singer for Kittanning, and Ellie Quinn, a typical twenty-seven-year-old.

To the outside world, these two Eleanors were inseparable. To her, they didn't even exist in the same universe.

The last guy she had dated had been an actor. James had loved the relationship. Moreover, he had loved what it did to her name value. And then, they broke up. The logistics of that relationship were simply impossible. The band had been on tour while he was filming in Europe. It was too complicated to connect. James had been more heartbroken over the breakup than Eleanor.

A breakup song. That was a lot easier to write. A deep part of her soul almost thrived on the loss and the darkness that came with a breakup. It caused a creative rush. She had once heard of a singer who wrote an entire album the night her husband left her. That was the type of love Eleanor wanted. The kind of love that demanded to be mourned in the best way love can be, through good music. She had not had a passion worthy of that in years.

She thought about people she knew who were in love.

She thought about James and his wife.

She thought about her parents.

Her older brother.

Jenny and Chip.

She started to pick out a slow, longing melody.

And just like that, the words came.

(Art)
All of my life
You've been by my side,
And now I get to call you home.
Life on the road
It calls my name
But in my mind, I go running home to you
At the end of the day.

(Eleanor)
Life on the road
It calls my name.
It's like something I can't explain.
To do this with you
Is a dream come true.
You are my home at the end of the day x2

(Both)
It's the thought of you
That gets me through
Each and every long day.
The hope of tomorrow
Another day in your arms
Is enough to numb my pain.

(Eleanor)
Oh, I wish
You would come home
Home to me

Oh, I wish
You would come home
Home to me

(Both)
Because no one sees me
Quite like you do.
No one else knows my pain.
So I will come home/Won't you come home
Home to me.

August 27th

Cynthia

This feels like the worst hangover I have had in my entire life," I said, rolling over on Kristy's couch. My newly shortened hair stuck out in every direction.

"Wow, that must mean a lot, coming from a pop star like you."

I could barely muster a laugh.

"You need to get outside. Look, it's sunny. This is a rare gift in Seattle. Get outside and get some fresh air, enjoy the freedom of the Wild West! You will drive yourself crazy if you only move from the bed to the couch every day. Remember, there *is* a world happening outside of your mind. And outside of my apartment," she tacked on for good measure.

I had been living at Kristy's for three days now. I had cut my hair. I had thrown my phone in the garbage, literally, because I could not deal with the constant ringing. I didn't know how to break it to James that I wasn't coming back. So instead, I said nothing.

Someone had once told me that the best way to get over a breakup was with a clean break. Cut all contact. Delete their number. Do not attempt to run into them, don't like their posts on Instagram. Cut it all off. This seemed, at the time, like an easy thing to do. It wasn't. Every bone in my body felt like it was breaking, and every muscle ached. Ignoring everyone felt like a more significant betrayal than leaving had.

But Kristy agreed that this was what I had to do. If I responded to anyone, even Jenny, explaining why I had left or that I was okay, it would ruin everything. They would find me, and I would be back on the stage before people even started questioning the bronchitis story.

So, I went for a walk.

Really, if I wanted to point the finger at the culprit for what happened next, it would be at Kristy's prodding that made me leave the house and buy the magazine.

I hadn't meant to buy it. I was never one to buy tabloids; my friends were mostly celebrities. If they had news, I'd want them to pick up the phone and call me. I was not going to turn to a magazine to see who was possibly pregnant.

For the record, I had apparently been trying to hide a pregnancy on our last tour. If someone hadn't sent me a link to the article, I never would have known I was expecting. Why even buy a pregnancy test when you could read the announcement for your upcoming bundle of joy in a magazine?

The first three days at Kristy's, I felt like an undercover spy. After dropping me off at her apartment, she went out and got hair dye. We cut and chopped my hair into a short bob—Eleanor Quinn had always been known for her cascade of golden, effortlessly-wavy hair. Kristy then went out and bought a whole new wardrobe for me, clothes that resembled nothing I had had in my previous closet. I was so used to the royal blues and chic French lines my stylist chose to bring out my eyes and showcase my tall, lean body. I was used to everything I wore, every way I styled my hair, to be curated for me, the Eleanor Quinn the world wanted to see. Kristy had brought home a wardrobe I could only describe as an explosion of hope in every shade imaginable. There were golden beanies and sunny scarves and slouchy off-the-shoulder tops in a very trendy shade of mustard. There was even a pair of chartreuse pants. Nothing in this haul was like anything I was used to. And I loved it.

All of this so that I could go outside without being recognized.

Leaving her apartment now felt like how I imagine a bear felt crawling out of its den after hibernation. Granted, my hibernation had only lasted three days. This was also the first time in recent years that I was not afraid that I would be stopped for an autograph or picture or that I had to be on the lookout for paparazzi. I was free to go to the store, just like an ordinary person.

Even the covering of my new hair and clothes and the lack of stage makeup couldn't dilute my paranoia. I looked over my shoulder at almost every other step. I was so afraid of being caught. Someone could figure out that I had escaped to Seattle, although just a small handful of people knew I was missing. I tried to rack my brain to remember if I had ever mentioned to anyone that my cousin had moved to Seattle. I had no memory of it coming up in conversation, but that didn't mean I hadn't mentioned it in passing at some point. I couldn't be too careful. I really didn't want to ruin my new freedom on my first day out of the apartment.

I wandered around Kristy's neighborhood without knowing where I was going. What do people do when they say they are going out to run errands?

I found my way into a Safeway. This new life was the perfect opportunity to finally study the art of baking. This would be my new hobby, I decided, walking into the overly air-conditioned store. I would learn how to bake and put all my extra energy into becoming a master baker. It would at least give me something to do.

It was in the checkout line, armed with the supplies I assumed were needed to make a cake, when I spotted the magazine. I didn't even mean to look at the display rack, but out of the corner of my eye, I couldn't help but notice my sparkling onesie on the front cover of this week's *People* magazine. My hands were frozen over my mouth in shock. Pieces of my hair were stuck to my stage makeup. I could tell the picture had been taken near the end of the show, which was even more apparent when I spotted him in the picture next to me, down on one knee.

"Fairy Tales Do Come True!" the headline screamed at me.

I had to buy it. I needed to know what was being said about my life.

I ripped it open as soon as I got back to Kristy's, abandoning my cake-baking supplies on the counter.

The first thing I noticed was how deceiving the picture was. I looked happy; we looked happy. I was a better actress than I thought.

Underneath the illusion of happiness, you could tell there was a layer of surprise. That was genuine. I had had no idea it was going to happen—and in Denver of all places. I looked closely at the other person in the shot. His face looked happy as well, but it also shone with hope and expectation. His true colors must have been magically Photoshopped out.

I thought back to my own memory of that moment.

I had not felt happiness.

I had been shocked. I still felt shocked. Even seeing it, my brain refused to accept this reality.

I could not get over the deceptiveness of the picture. In reality, I had felt suffocated, as if I was suddenly an animal trapped in a cage with 20,000 people looking at me. They were all waiting for my obvious yes.

I had to say yes. Well, Eleanor Quinn had to say yes. She couldn't disappoint her fans. Not right in front of them like this. I had been stuck inside a life that had been constructed around me. I had not chosen any of this: the setlist, my outfit, or to be in Denver that night. And I definitely hadn't picked this proposal.

I remembered my head nodding, slightly, once up and down.

I remembered being picked up off my feet and twirled around the stage in fake joy.

I remembered confetti falling from the sky.

I remembered the deafening roar of 20,000 people, louder than ever.

And then I remembered crying.

The tears had been real. The onlookers assumed they were tears of joy, but they were not. It was panic and sadness at realizing that this life was not mine at all. Sure, I was living it, but that was only because they needed someone to play the part of Eleanor Quinn.

The tabloid article told the story of our whirlwind romance. It went on and on about how our love was so unexpected, a surprise to everyone around us.

A source close to the couple said, "When they first got together, I was a little shocked, but then, the more I saw them together, the more I thought about it, the more I realized that the signs had pointed to this all along. I don't think there have ever been two people more perfect for each other."

I wanted to gag. Who was the "source?" I felt the sudden urge to call Jess. This was the type of story that we would have spent hours laughing about.

Except for the fact that this event had so many witnesses. People who were otherwise in no way involved in my personal life. This was not just another engagement or pregnancy rumor. Twenty thousand people had seen what was now being deemed America's dream proposal, and there were photos to prove it.

I desperately missed my best friend. I felt awful for vanishing without telling her. We usually talked these sorts of things through. We tried to be sounding boards for each other. And I had just made a significant life change without telling her. I was worried about what she would think when she heard the story. She had known my true feelings about the relationship, and I hoped that she knew me well enough to know that I would have at least given her a heads up if I had changed my mind about him.

Then again, I had vanished off the face of the earth (successfully, hopefully) and had neglected to tell her. Hopefully, that gave her a good clue as to my real feelings.

I kept on reading the article. It gushed over how happy we were together, how we were the ultimate power couple. The band was delighted. Everyone was supportive. *Everyone, that is, except for the "bride-to-be,"* I thought to myself. But who cared what she thought, anyway?

The last line on the page glared at me like a neon billboard.

"Eleanor Quinn has not been seen since her engagement. Is she lovesick? Her manager has said that she is battling bronchitis and is expected to return to the stage any night now. 'Knowing Eleanor, she will be back on the stage before you know it. We are just waiting for her doctor to give us the go-ahead. Eleanor would never do anything to let her fans down. That would be denying a part of who she really is.'"

It was as if he had said that in hopes that I would read the quote. Eleanor would *never* do anything to let down her fans. My stomach twisted.

I was rereading the article for the fifth time when Kristy got home from work.

"What happened?" It must have been clear from my face that something was off. "Were you able to leave the house today?"

"I'm letting everyone down," I sobbed. It felt like the world was crashing down on me.

"Why do you say that?"

I pushed the magazine over to her.

She said nothing but instead pulled me in for a hug.

A few minutes later, she spoke. "I am always here if you want to talk about what happened. We don't have to. I just want you to know that you have a friend, and you don't have to go through this alone."

That only made me cry harder. I didn't even know where to begin. I didn't know how to explain the internal conflict that was raging in my mind.

There were only two options going forward. I could start over, stay in hiding, and let down all the people I loved, or I could go back and suffer with a smile on my face, playing the role that the world told me to play.

I thought about it over and over. I couldn't go back. Something in me had snapped that night in Denver, and the person I saw in the picture was no longer who I was. I couldn't go back to being that girl. I couldn't get on the stage and smile as if to say everything was okay when I was dying inside. That would feel like the ultimate betrayal of myself and of my fans.

I would never be able to get on that stage again. Eleanor Quinn might never have been able to disappoint her fans, but that was no longer who I was. I was Cynthia: a worldly, organized baker who was not musical in any way. Cynthia was a writer. Cynthia was just a girl from western Pennsylvania who had moved to Seattle to fulfill her dream of moving out west. She was everything that Eleanor could never be.

I would will that to become true.

All my career, I had been trained to create a story that I wished was true. I thought of *Home,* of the world I had created to make that song real. This was my opportunity to make those imaginary worlds a reality. This was my chance to rewrite my story. No label, no James telling me what to do or what to create.

But there was still a feeling of loss for the person I had been just three days before.

I didn't know how to explain this to my cousin. She had been able to make all her own choices in life: where she went to college, what she majored in, her first job. As soon as Kittanning had released its first album, my freedom of choice was gone. I had known that I would never go to college or have a career. It was my job.

At the time, being famous had felt like everything I had ever wanted. I had never loved school anyway. I had always dreamed of being in a band. This was everything that I had ever dreamed of, and every dream came with some sacrifices, right?

Younger Eleanor could never have grasped what that loss and surrender of freedom would actually mean for her life.

Looking over at my cousin, I felt a twinge of jealousy. Maybe I should never have joined the band. What if I had gone to college and just played in bars for fun on the weekend? I would have been able to talk about making an album like it was an unachievable dream. That would have preserved some of the romance of it. I could have married my college sweetheart and been the cool mom who let her kids listen to rock and roll.

Maybe it wasn't too late for that. I was young. Who was to say I couldn't start over?

"I want to be able to choose what happens next," I finally said. "I have lived my whole life being told who I am supposed to be. I want to decide what happens next."

"Great. I like this plan!" Kristy said in a cheerful, supportive tone. "What can I do to help you?"

"Can you help me apply to college?

January 3rd

Eleanor

You wrote us a bloody love song!?" Art's perfectly symmetrical face was contorted in an angry grimace.

Art and Eleanor happened to show up at the studio at the same time the next afternoon and were now crammed in the elevator together.

"First off, don't say bloody. You're not British, and it makes you sound like a tool," Eleanor responded curtly.

"Oh, you didn't see? I've been dating Korine; she was in New York working on a project, and we ended up getting drinks. It was in *Page Six*! Anyways, her vocabulary must be rubbing off on me."

"I don't read *Page Six*," Eleanor ground out, "I figured if something important was happening in your life, you would call and tell me about it, not wait for me to find out in some trashy magazine." In truth, Eleanor *had* heard that Art and Korine had been spotted together. At this point, Art had been spotted with almost every single model who entered the city limits. It was hard for her to keep up with who he was "dating" now. Besides, it wasn't her business who he dated. As long as it didn't affect the band, she didn't care.

She had heard about him and Korine because one of her cousins was obsessed with the model and had sent Eleanor the article, asking if she could get Korine's autograph. Eleanor had said she would see what she could do, knowing full well that as soon as the band started touring, Art would have moved on . . . if they even lasted that long.

"Ellie, you are missing the point. You wrote us a love song? Why would you do that? The album is finished!"

"James told me I had to. The label wanted another love song on the album."

"You are kidding me." Clearly, Art's conversation with James hadn't gone as smoothly as Ellie had hoped.

"Do you honestly think that I was planning to spend my Monday afternoon penning a duet about our deep love for each other?"

"Why could you not have just written a song for you to sing on your own? I thought I was done recording. I would have happily let you have a track to yourself if it meant that I didn't have to spend another day in this studio."

They both knew that was a lie. Art was not one to share his spotlight, and that meant Eleanor would never have a song to herself on any of their albums. Something fans had pointed out. Not that he was selfish with who got to sing, but there were comments wishing the band would let Eleanor sing more. Occasionally, she got a guitar solo without any pushback. Every time that happened, it felt like a major win.

"So, what, are you like in love with me now or something?" His piercing eyes narrowed in her direction.

"Art, writing songs is my job."

"That doesn't answer the question."

"Art, there will never be a world where I am in love with you."

"Okay, good, just making sure. I don't want to have to break your heart."

"Bummer, think of all the wonderful break-up songs I could write to kick off my solo career with."

"Yes, I am sure you would have a solo career," he said with an eye roll as the elevator doors opened.

She would have an amazing solo career, she thought to herself.

She had tried, a few years ago, to get the rest of the band's feeling regarding Art. They were loyal to the end. Jenny, the drummer, had twitched her eye slightly, which Eleanor correctly took to mean she had a less than positive opinion of him. But Chip just went off about how talented he was.

Eleanor knew then that if she ever did decide to break away from Kittanning, she would be making the journey alone. They could find another female singer literally anywhere. This was New York, for goodness's sake. Half of the women in the city were aspiring singers. The other half were waiting for their big Broadway break, also singers.

"Finally," James said as they entered the studio. "Okay, we just need you to record this one last song, and then, I promise you, the album is done, closed, off to the press!"

She hated the way James said, "just." We "just" need you to record this, as if this were not a tall ask.

"We thought it might be fun to have a piano, really make it more like a sad, lovesick ballad. Nothing over-produced, just stripped back, the two of you and a piano."

"Just the two of us and a piano, the title of our next love song, aye, Ellie?" Art said with a wink.

He was always like this in front of James, playing up to whatever he wanted. He painted Eleanor to be the problem child.

"Only if we can do an album of duets, like Dolly Parton and Porter Wagoner." She replied sarcastically.

"You joke," James said, looking at me, "But that could be a hit."

"Over my dead body," she said to him under her breath.

Later that night, Eleanor met her friend Jess at their favorite wine bar. "He said that he wanted it to seem like we were sharing a microphone," she said, a mixture of laughter and anger.

"You're kidding. Do you think anyone will believe that? I mean, you are a good actress, don't get me wrong, but you don't think people will actually believe a love song about the two of you?" Jess had met Eleanor at their favorite wine bar after Eleanor was finally freed from the studio.

Jess and Eleanor had met in the bathroom at the Grammy's a few years ago and had been attached at the hip ever since. Jess had broken away from her overbearing first-generation Pakistani-American parents. She marched to the tune of her own drum, never giving in to the pressure of believing she needed to be a part of a band to have a career. She thought and knew she could stand on her own. And she did. They each cherished the friendship for so many reasons, the main one being neither woman had to explain anything to the other. They both understood the unspoken rules of life as a woman in this industry. There was no need to qualify or explain. They just understood.

"No, I mean, the whole thing felt so fake. Like no amount of good acting would be able to make it really seem like I love Art. Most days, I'm just happy that people buy our 'friendship.'"

Eleanor's phone beeped.

Get ready; Home is going to be the next single! -J

She looked to Jess as if she could have thrown her phone across the crowded bar.

"What?" Jess asked, and then the realization hit her: "Oh gosh, they are going to release it as a single, aren't they?"

"Yes, ugh, this was supposed to be a final touch at the end of a great album, like a nice epilogue. The rest of the album is trendy, upbeat; this was supposed to be the final piece to just round it out. You do not release the rounding-out song as a single."

"I mean, I would say I hope that it flops, but let's be honest, if you want the album to do well, you need this to go well."

"I cannot believe this. Art is going to be so smug about this. I do not want to deal with him right now."

"Maybe this won't be as bad as you think. Maybe people will think it is a song written just about people in love, not you two specifically."

"Jess, I am the only credit on the lyrics; they are going to assume that I either wrote the song about Art or that I am in a relationship."

"Why are those the only two options? You are a writer; this is what you do. Surely people have to believe that you can draw on other experiences to write?"

"Yeah, of course, the press *always* gives us the benefit of the doubt."

"Okay, fair point." She took a sip of her drink. "So, what are you going to do?"

"I guess I'll just play it off as something I wrote about someone else. I'm sure I can come up with some story of love, inevitably resulting in heartbreak, because I do not have the energy to fake date someone right now, and then I will say that this song came to me in the middle of that mysterious whirlwind relationship. Something sappy like that."

"Good plan. So, who *did* you write the song about?" The words coming from anyone else would have felt like an accusation. But that was just Jess.

"This is going to sound so weird, but I wrote it about James."

"You cannot be in love with James. That's like a weird Stockholm syndrome situation!"

"Ew, no, you didn't let me finish; I wrote it about James and his wife. There are other people I know whose relationships I admire, like Chip and Jenny. But James and his wife are by far my favorite couple on tour. Like if for some reason, she isn't with us for a leg of the tour, they are on the phone with each other all the time—and not out of obligation but because they genuinely care about what the other one is doing. Like, they tell each other what they had to eat that day; they overshare about every detail of their lives. It is, like, the cutest, most authentically-nauseating love story I have ever seen."

"Awwww, James!"

"I know! It's the stuff people dream about. And, on top of it all, they're actually happy. If the cameras are rolling or not."

"Well, good for him. Everyone should have a love like that."

"I know. I am happy for him."

"For sure, and I am not at all jealous that he found someone who is willing to put up with his crazy schedule and inhuman hours."

"And they're both happy?"

January 20th

Two Fridays later, Eleanor woke up with a jolt.

Release day.

She lived for these days.

It felt like the moment before you open the door to a party. There was a deep-rooted feeling that something good was behind the door, and there was great anticipation of what was to come.

"Home," the label decided, was going to be the last single released before the album. The song had grown on her. Even if Eleanor didn't love the idea of singing a love song with Art, the feelings of release day remained the same.

Something she created, something she wrote, was being released into the world. There was something so intimate and vulnerable about the release of music. Something so personal thrown out into the world, asking to be critiqued, judged, and played on repeat.

Eleanor lived for this type of rush.

She clicked open her phone.

RELEASE DAY!!! XXXXX A message from Jess read.

Don't forget you need to be outside to meet the car by 11, from James. He didn't like to count his chickens before they were hatched. He was very superstitious and wouldn't use the words single, album, or release on the day of any release. He didn't want to jinx it. She knew deep down he was celebrating. They had all worked hard for this day.

Eleanor had called him earlier in the week and told him the truth about the song. In true James fashion, he didn't say anything for a while and then finally mustered a, "Well, I will tell Sheryl that. She will be very honored." And then he hung up the phone.

Eleanor bounced around her apartment as she got ready. The joy was floating through her. She clicked open Spotify. There it was, smiling back at her. It had been added to that week's new release playlist. This feeling would never get old. There was nothing more joyful than seeing hard work pay off, shared with the rest of the world.

GUYS!!! People are sharing the song like crazy! Jenny wrote in the band's group chat.

Good job, you guys!! We did it! from Chip.

So thankful to get to work with you guys! responded Eleanor. For the most part, this was true. She did love Chip and Jenny.

See you guys at the release party tonight! Jenny responded quickly. She was always the first to plan a celebration.

Eleanor noticed another message from Jenny, sent just to her.

E, do you think people will think you and Art are dating? I mean, like, I know you two and that would never happen, duh, but listening to the song again, it really sounds like you are into each other??

Eleanor didn't know what to say. Her biggest fear was being spelled out by one of her closest friends.

I mean, I don't think so. I will just say that I wrote it about someone else. For all they know, it could be about Chip and me.

Yeah, in your dreams.

Jenny and Chip had been together since high school. In another life, they could have been Bonnie and Clyde with their All-American good looks and perfect chemistry. They were so in love that it made Eleanor a little sick.

33

Don't worry. This is not going to be an ABBA situation. Eleanor had felt like she needed to add that assurance.

For years, people had been waiting for Eleanor and Art to fall in love. To the outside world, this made sense. Eleanor was tall and blonde, slightly reserved but clearly talented. Art was handsome and charismatic. Together, they looked nothing short of a power couple, as if they were created to be together. However, Jenny had expressed many times her fears about being the next ABBA. The four members of the iconic Swedish group had paired off and gotten married, only to get divorced a few years later. The band broke up a year after the last couple divorced. Jenny was willing to do everything in her power to prevent Kittanning from being the next ABBA. She and Chip had gone to intensive couples counseling before they got married, not because she thought they needed it, but because she wanted to make sure that if they broke up, it would not be the end of her career.

Life was not easy for a female drummer. Also, looking at history, the men of the ABBA break-up, in the eyes of Jenny, did much better than their ex-wives. See the movie *Mamma Mia* for reference. The only time Jenny had watched *Mamma Mia*, she left the theater crying, fearful of how she would be written in history if she and Chip separated. She had already imagined him writing a musical using their music without her.

Eleanor doubted this would ever happen. Jenny and Chip were one of the happiest and—more importantly—healthiest and stable couples she had ever met.

Dancing around her bedroom to a playlist that had been created based on their song, Eleanor grabbed the preselected outfit for the day. It was nice, she reasoned with herself, that she never needed to pick out her own clothes. Sure, she had a say in what she wore, but every piece was hand-selected and very calculated.

Today was an all-black jumpsuit, which reminded Eleanor of Olivia Newton John's look in *Grease*.

Her dancing was interrupted by Julia, her hair and makeup lady, who showed up a little before nine.

"Congrats on the song!" she said as she bounced into Eleanor's apartment. "It made me want to fall in love!"

"Thank you! I know, me too."

"What do you mean, 'me too?' I figured that this song was your way to tell the world that you and Art were finally a thing?"

Julia was dead serious. Eleanor had only known her for a year, and it was clear Julia didn't really understand the full drama behind Eleanor and Art's relationship. She had never actually seen them together, and Eleanor was very selective about those with whom she shared her issues with Art. In her mind, worse than an ABBA situation would be one where the world knew the truth about Eleanor and Art. No one wanted to go see a band who not-so-secretly hated each other. She was a good actress. She was willing to fake it for the success of Kittanning.

"Oh, no! Art and I are not together. It was just a song."

"But you wrote it, right? The guy on the radio in the car ride over said that you had sole credit on the lyrics. He said that could only mean one thing: You wrote the song about Art."

"Or," I said quickly, "I wrote it from the perspective of two people who are in love. That is what writers do, after all; we put ourselves into the perspective of others."

"Yeah, I guess that's true. I guess I just wanted to believe that a fairy tale ending was possible."

"I mean, it totally is possible. Art and I will never be a couple; that's impossible. But a fairy tale ending. That's what the song is about to me, the hope of finding someone who makes anywhere in the world feel like home."

Julia's face could not hide her disappointment. Eleanor wondered to herself how many times she was going to have to explain this to people.

The car was outside of Eleanor's building exactly two minutes before eleven. Inside was James, looking stressed.

"You don't look like someone who manages a band who just dropped a charting-topping single! Come on, James, lighten up!" Eleanor said as she slid into the backseat of the SUV.

In response, James gave her a worried smile.

"James, are you okay? Did something happen?" Panic rushed through Eleanor's veins. What if someone had died? How would she be able to be peppy at a release party and a day full of interviews knowing that someone she loved so much was suffering?

"No, no, it's nothing like that," he said in a hurry. "I have something to tell you. I just need you to know that this was not my decision; this is coming from the top. Don't shoot the messenger, deal?"

"Okay, I promise," Eleanor nodded nervously.

"The label wants you and Art to date." He rushed through the words quickly before Eleanor could cut him off. "You obviously don't actually have to date him, but with the reception of the song, this is what the people are asking for. The world wants you two to be in love. At least for a while, for the sake of PR for the song, the album, and the tour."

Eleanor was momentarily stunned. There was no way they were having this discussion.

"You cannot do this to me." Eleanor pleaded.

"The label thinks it will help sales. The world wants you two to be in love, and is that really such a bad thing? The world needs more love."

"Is that really such a bad thing? James, do you know *anything* about my relationship with Art?"

"I know that things have not always been easy for you with him, but you just need to fake it in front of the cameras. Off-screen, live your life like normal. They just want shots of you leaving his apartment building in the morning a few times a week, you need to act in love with each other when being interviewed, that sort of thing."

"James, you can't be serious. This goes beyond my job. It's my life! You're asking me to give up my life."

"No, I am not asking. I am telling you to fake date your band-mate for a few months."

"You are asking me to lie to my fans, to the world, and to put my personal life on hold."

"Don't be a drama queen, Ellie."

"You know this means that I won't actually be able to date, right? If I am 'dating' Art, then I won't be able to date anyone else. You really want me to hit pause on my future?"

"When was the last time you dated someone?"

"I could be dating someone now. You don't know that."

"If you are dating someone, and you have kept it a secret, even from me, then you will be able to fake date Art during this press tour and keep dating your alleged 'secret boyfriend,' no problem."

Eleanor could have punched him. He knew that he had won the argument—if that even counted as an argument—and there was nothing Eleanor could do about it. At the end of the day, more than anything, more than she wanted to be in a relationship with someone she truly liked, she wanted what was best for the band.

"Fine."

"Great," James said victoriously. "We are picking him up next, and we are going to go over the story of how you two finally got together."

"James, I have a girlfriend. I've been dating Korine, remember?" Art said smugly as soon as James finished laying out the plan moments later.

"Oh, come on, Art, you and I both know that you are just hooking up with her; you were going to ditch her as soon as the tour started anyway."

"You don't know that; it could have actually been love!"

"Was it?"

"Of course not. But have you seen how hot she is? And you expect the world to believe that I broke up with her for *Eleanor*?" He gestured over to Eleanor, who was glaring at him from her seat in the now overly-cramped car.

"You are a pig," she shot back.

"Get over yourself." Art said flatly.

"Both of you get over yourselves," James spoke up before a fight could break out mid car ride. "I know this is weird, and you both think it sucks, but it is for the good of the album. People want to know they are listening to songs sung by people who actually like each other. I need you to put your personal issues with each other on the back burner for just like nine months, pretend to be in love, and then you can go back to hating each other for all I care. But I swear, if I hear one whisper in the press that you two don't get along, I will come for you both. Now, let's get some details straight."

The rest of the car ride was relatively quiet as James described the history of Eleanor and Art's love.

"What are we supposed to say to Chip and Jenny?" Eleanor asked.

"I've already spoken to them. They are on board." James said without elaborating.

So, this is what it is going to be like, thought Eleanor.

"Are you guys ready to play nice?" James said as the car rolled to a stop.

•◦◦◦◦◦•

There is so much more to releasing a song than actually uploading the song. If a song is going to be a success, there is a large amount of press work that needs to go into it. The twenty-four hours after it releases, according to James, are the most important.

On the day of the single "Home's" release, James had scheduled a full slate of interviews before the celebration later that night. They were first scheduled to be interviewed by "Rolling Stone." He had designed this interview to come out before their album so that people would be impatiently waiting for the full album to drop.

The mood of those in the car with James was grim, to say the least, when they arrived at the studio where the interview was to take place.

"You two at least need to pretend to be happy," James said sternly. He pushed them closer together. "You need to walk in together like you are a couple. This starts now."

Roughly, Art reached over and took Eleanor's hand in one of his own baby-smooth hands.

"Perfect, this looks super believable," James said with an eye roll.

When they walked through the door, Eleanor's face immediately turned red. She could not help it. She knew that all eyes were on her, and not for a reason she approved.

Jenny shot her a sympathetic look. Eleanor knew that her ABBA fears were screaming loudly in her head. They would be talking about this tomorrow when they could have a free moment together.

It had been so long since she had been a part of a couple, Eleanor had forgotten how she was supposed to act. How long was she supposed to hold Art's hand? At what point was it weird and unnatural. As they sat next to each other on the couch, was she supposed to snuggle up next to him, or did that look too forced?

They had a few minutes before the interviewer arrived. Eleanor only had a few minutes to run over the story again in her head, a few moments to make sure that she looked as natural as possible curled up next to someone that she could not stand to be around.

"Yes, this looks right." James said approvingly as Eleanor hesitatingly draped one leg over Art's.

It might have looked right to him, but to Eleanor, it felt like writing with her left hand.

"Oh my gosh!" Meredith had interviewed the band a few times before, and she was always over the top. Eleanor could not think of a time when her hair was not done perfectly and her clothes looked as if she has just stepped off the cover of a magazine. This added to the voraciousness of her personality. Today, Eleanor realized that George must have hand-picked her for that very reason. She was going to write the perfect over-the-top piece about the season's hottest new romance.

"You guys," she said, once she had finally settled a little, "I heard the song, and I just knew—this was your way of announcing your love to the world, and I was so worried I was going to come here today, and you were going to deny it, but oh my gosh, does this," she gestured to Eleanor and Art's posture on the couch, "mean that you are official?"

Eleanor felt Art's leg tense underneath hers. At least this felt uncomfortable for him as well.

James laughed, "Okay, let's get started. You are the first stop of our day, Meredith." He was clearly appealing to her ego.

"Oh, believe me, you picked the perfect person to break this story, if that is, in fact, what this is," she winked dramatically.

"Are we on the record?" Eleanor voiced timidly. They had practiced this. Eleanor was never timid about interviews, but James thought that this would be more believable if she came off bashful. James also wanted the story to be told by Eleanor. Because Meredith was a woman, James had reasoned. He thought that speaking woman-to-woman would add an extra layer to the story.

"Just like a conversation between best girlfriends," he had said in the car.

"Yes, of course! Spill all!" Meredith flipped on her recorder.

And then, for the first time in her career, Eleanor lied her way through an interview.

This would not be the last.

August 27th

Cynthia

Okay, so I am not saying that going to college is a bad idea. I am team 'go to college,' but just to play the devil's advocate, you realize that a university campus is a really public place, right? Like, you could be recognized, and then what would you do? When was the last time you spent a large amount of time in public without a security guard? Would you actually use your name? And what would you study?"

Kristy was pacing around the house. She was a pacer, I learned. Kristy's fears did not mean she thought I was dumb or even wrong. Kristy wanted to rationalize her way to alignment with my side, to see things from my perspective before making up her mind. She had always been like this, even when we were kids.

When we were ten, we had invented a whole little town into my backyard. We had elected Kristy the town's judge, a job which she took very seriously. Every charge that came across her imaginary desk, she thought about with great detail. She wanted to see whatever the issue was from every side. We were rarely able to pass any laws because she spent too much time debating with herself. It was not a very productive government.

Clearly, she had not changed.

I, on the other hand, had always been more of an irrational decision-maker. This was most recently demonstrated by my choice to get on a bus pointed to Seattle with no real plan.

"I think I want to study history. As a kid, I remember thinking that it would be fun to be a teacher. And I really like history. I could see myself really liking it." I made this all up on the spot. Yes, as a kid, I had played teacher, but I had not actually thought about being a teacher until the words came out of my mouth just then. "And I could hire a security guy. But I doubt that anyone will recognize me. I'll fly under the radar."

Kristy rolled her eyes. "This isn't the Disney channel. Do you really think you can pull off Hannah Montana? Come on, Ellie, this is not realistic."

"People have doppelgängers. Also, as of now, I go by Cynthia."

Kristy stopped pacing to pin me with a stare. "You *actually* expect me to call you Cynthia?"

"I guess you don't have to when we are in the house, but I am serious about starting over. If I want to blend in, I can't go by Ellie or Eleanor anymore. I can't have a name that sounds close either; I don't want to raise suspicions."

"Okay, so I guess this means that this is a sure thing, right? Like . . . you're not going back?"

"Kristy, I can't go back. I can't put myself through that again. I mean, what the world saw was only half the story. If I go back, I would be betraying myself. I had to put my entire life on hold, and I can't do that anymore. I can't live my life trying to become who they want me to be. I want my future back, and I honestly think this is the only way to do that. I need a clean break."

"Okay, then count me in. Whatever you need me to do. I am assuming that you are going to be my permanent roommate, then?"

"Is that okay? I mean, I can find something else if that is easier. I don't want to invade your life."

"*Mi casa es tu casa.*" Kristy chuckled to herself. "Really. I didn't need the spare bedroom anyway. I had already been thinking about finding a roommate to keep me company."

"Are you sure?" I did not want to be the houseguest that never leaves.

"Yes, 100 percent. Please stay."

"Okay, so housing, check! I need to figure out how to get money out of my bank account without it being suspicious. I also need a new cell phone number. I didn't really have much of a plan formulated other than get to Seattle. Aside from that, all I know about getting a new identity I learned from movies."

"Helpful. I am sure those are super realistic."

Two hours, a new cell phone, and a few glasses of wine later, we had the framework of a plan.

"Okay, so you could do a bank transfer to another account, like a shell account. But I think you can only really transfer $2,000 at a time without being flagged. So, I think if you slowly transferred money, it wouldn't be suspicious. But there is no way you could pull out money that slowly and pay for classes."

"What if I just took one class at a time? That would be cheaper, right? Then I wouldn't have to pay for a whole semester at once?"

"I think that would be doable."

"More than anything, I just need something to do. Like I miss writing and going to the studio and rehearsals. I feel like I have lost my purpose. At least if I had a class to go to, even if it were only a few times a week, I would have something to do."

"Have you been writing?"

"Not really."

"El—I mean, Cynthia," she said with a wink, "In your whole life, I have never seen you without a piece of paper within arm's reach. Writing is a part of who you are. I don't want you to leave that behind just because you are not in Kittanning anymore. Maybe you could sign up for a writing class!"

"Yeah, that's a good idea."

The truth was, I had been writing. I couldn't stop. The words felt as if they had to be written down, or they would consume my soul. I knew realistically there was no way for the words I had written to actually be put out into the world. I had lost my outlet. I doubted that any label would pick up a lyricist they had never heard of and who, on paper, seemed to have no writing experience or training. I knew, sadly, that these words were just for me.

We found a writing class at Seattle University. English 2050, an intro to creative writing class. I had never written anything other than lyrics, so this could be a good change of pace.

Maybe I could become the next great American novelist.

Or, maybe, I could find an outlet to share my story. This could be an excellent way to process. People write fiction to process their lives through the lens of an imagined narrative, right?

That was what I assumed, at least.

The class was going to start the following Monday. Kristy approved of me taking the course only if I had some sort of security. She reasoned that, by Monday, there would be a higher likelihood that my disappearance would be leaked. She figured that an Eleanor Quinn look-alike, even with shorter, seemingly natural red hair, was bound to raise some suspicions.

I had never hired anyone before. To my knowledge, James had always taken care of this for us. New security team members popped up like magic. It was a system I knew nothing about.

"Okay, I have a co-worker whose husband is a bouncer at a bar on Capitol Hill. Maybe if you made him a better offer, he would be willing to be your security team for the quarter instead. At least until you find a more permanent thing. Do you want me to talk to her?"

"Do you mind? Like, is that weird? And you won't tell him who I am?"

"Your secret is safe with me."

"Great, let's call him up!"

I wasn't sure if I was supposed to interview him or if he was interviewing me.

The bouncer's name was Randy. His head glistened under the light, and warm eyes sized me up thoroughly. He was probably in his early thirties and just by looking at him, I knew why he had a successful career as a bouncer. He was at least six feet, six inches tall with dark chocolate skin and massive tree trunk arms. He must spend most of his day in the gym. I was a peanut next to him.

It made me feel safe.

"So, how do you envision this working?" Randy said. I realized I had not spoken for several minutes. Kristy cleared her throat passive-aggressively in the corner as if to cue me to speak.

"Is it okay if we keep a really high level of privacy? You will need to sign an NDA."

"Sure."

"Great, my name is Cynthia. Also, I really don't want people to know that you are my security. I don't know if it is easier if we ignore each other, and you just always happen to have the same classes as me, or if we should play it off that we are friends?"

"What would make you the most comfortable?"

"I think if we just kept our distance. I just want to be able to fly under the radar."

"Okay."

I appreciated that he did not question my strange paranoid requests. I figured this meant that I wouldn't have to explain or justify myself to him. It would make my life a lot easier.

"Can you meet me here on Monday morning? We can take the bus together."

"You are not taking the bus," Kristy interjected quickly. "That is just asking to be spotted by someone who will recognize you."

"What else am I supposed to do? I don't drive." I retorted back.

"You can't drive, or you don't like to drive?"

"I can't. I never learned. When in my life would I have needed to learn how to drive? That was never a life skill I needed." I realized I was defensive. She had just asked a question.

Randy just looked at us both. I think he was debating if it was worth it to ask a clarifying question or not.

"Do I want to know?" He asked, finally, with a lot of caution.

"I've just always had a driver. That is all you need to know."

"Well, do you want me to be your driver as well? I do have *my* license." There was an undertone of sassiness in his voice that I really appreciated. I smiled. I missed bantering with people. I missed conversations that were more lighthearted than the ones I had been faced with the past week. It was nice to have someone tell a joke.

"Do you mind? I will cover your gas and mileage."

"Sure, no problem. This is Seattle, after all. Everyone carpools. We will blend right in."

I looked over at Kristy to ensure that we had her final approval. Her approval felt like the last barrier between me and freedom.

"Fine," she said finally.

With that, Randy was out the door promising to be five minutes early on Monday. He didn't want to be late for his first day of class, he said with a smirk.

"Okay, paranoid much?" I said to her as soon as he managed to squeeze his giant self out of our average-sized doorway.

"Yes, I am paranoid. How do you expect me to feel? You call me out of the blue a week ago, saying that you are on a bus heading to Seattle. You won't tell me what is going on. The press hasn't broken the story that you are missing yet, but you and I both know that it is only a matter of time before the wrong person says the right thing, and then what? Did you think you could just fade away, and no one would notice that you were gone? This is very stressful for me. I don't want anything to happen to you, and I don't want it to be my fault." She let out a breath. "Sorry, I have been holding that in for a long time. I just don't know what the right thing to do is."

I curled my feet under me in my seat. I didn't know how to answer my cousin.

"You are right. I am sorry. I didn't give you any warning, and I know that this is a big life change for you, too. I am safe. I promise. Obviously, my disappearance will eventually get out. I guess that I was just hoping that I was forgettable, that no one would really remember me or notice that I was gone. They could get another female singer for the band, or Jenny could even do it. She has a better voice than she lets on. I just wanted to live a life where I got to make my own choices; I wanted to be able to slip away. I don't know what the best thing to do is. I just know that I can't go back. And I don't know how to talk about it yet. I just need you to trust me. This is the best that I can do right now."

She nodded.

"Please trust me. This will be okay. I will be okay. I won't do anything stupid. If I wanted to do something dumb, I would have decided that now was the right time to get a driver's license and drive myself to class. I might not have thought everything through, but I am not reckless."

"Okay, I trust you."

"Do you want to do something fun this weekend? It is my last weekend of the summer!" I said with a wink. "What do you normally do on the weekends?"

"I usually just clean my house, go for a run, go out for drinks, hike . . . I don't know. Normal stuff."

"Let's do that, please. Can we do something normal? I can even see if Randy will be willing to sit close by. We could go out for drinks tomorrow night, my treat?"

"That seems like a very public thing to do."

"Come on! We have gone out for drinks together before! It's chill."

"Yes, but the last time we went out, you had a security detail, and paparazzi were waiting for us outside of the bar. That is not a normal Saturday night for me."

"Well, if we go this weekend, it is not likely that anyone will realize I am missing yet. This might be our only chance!" I was dying to get out of the house, to do something that I would typically do. I needed some semblance of normal activity.

"Fine. But I pick the bar, and you coordinate with Randy."

"Done!"

I don't think I had realized what it would feel like to be out. I felt as if I had left my house without pants on. I felt more exposed than I thought I would. I kept looking over my shoulder the whole way to the bar. I was convinced that someone was following the car. The thought of my newfound freedom being stripped away put me on an edge I had not expected.

It did not help things that James had tracked down Kristy's phone number this morning. I knew this was going to happen. While I had tried to emotionally prepare for this, I knew that he would call my parents. They could tell at least a partial truth; I was not with them. I trusted them to figure out a lie to not alert James to my presence in Seattle. They were better liars than Kristy. Plus, James knew how to get to my parents' house, so if he really wanted to, he could drop by and see for himself that I was not in western Pennsylvania.

At some point, I had told him about Kristy, and I was sure that at this point, he remembered that she lived in Seattle. Thankfully, Seattle was a big city, and more than one Kristy Quinn was living here. I knew because I had checked a few days ago.

But he found her number. And he called.

She hadn't answered the phone, she had been in the shower when he called. But he left a message and promised he would be calling back.

He sounded overwhelmed and stressed. But mostly, he sounded angry. I knew I was the cause of this. I had never meant to hurt James. That was just an unfortunate side effect of my more significant need to save myself. If I could have gotten out and spared James, I would have. But this was the only way. Someday, he would get that. Maybe.

Seattle was a big city, I reminded myself.

"Are you sure you want to do this?" Kristy said after I turned around to check if we were being followed for the eighteenth time.

"Yes, I want to do this. I need to do this. I love the apartment, but I need to be reminded that there is a world outside of it."

"Okay," she said as she pulled into a parking spot.

She had picked a bar in Ballard. We had gone to Ballard the last time I was in Seattle. I loved this area of the city. It wasn't the most popular area to go out on a Saturday night, but there were still enough people around to assure you that you had picked a good neighborhood for your night out.

We sat in the back corner of the bar; I noticed Randy and his wife already seated across the room. As soon as I saw him, I did relax a little more. It was going to be okay.

"So, tell me if you want to, did you love him?" Kristy asked, halfway into a glass of Bordeaux. She only drank red wine. It made me wonder how she trusted herself with the beautiful white couch in her living room.

I sipped my Vodka Collins.

Did I love him? This was a more complicated question than I realized. My gut said no, of course not, but the more I had been thinking about it in the past days, I realized that deep down, I might have. Not romantically.

"I don't know," I said after another long sip. "For so long, my response was automatic—I am madly in love with him. But that was what James had trained me to say. But now that I have some agency, and some say over my own words again, I don't know. I think I liked the idea of being in love with him. Maybe I just liked the idea of being in love. Like it sounds like the right thing to do. It made so much sense on paper, but there were so many hidden layers to it. If I am honest, we are both different people in real life than when we are in front of the camera. When I am not in front of a camera, I feel like a more likable, normal person. I liked who he was on the camera, but as soon as the camera turned off, and the faces turned away . . ." I had to stop talking. I wasn't sure how to say what I needed to say without risking slandering the band.

And then I realized I wasn't in the band anymore. I was free. I didn't have to worry about how my comments would negatively affect my career. That career was dead the moment I got on the bus and stopped returning anyone's phone calls. It was already ruined. I was free to say whatever I wanted. I was free to say whatever I needed.

Kristy set down her glass. "Like was this a setup thing? Or how did that even happen? If you don't like a guy, you know that you have the right to not date him, right?"

"Yes, it was a setup, but it was more complicated than that. I didn't really have a choice. Well, that is not true. I had some choice. I could have written a crappy song, to begin with."

"Wait, this happened because of the song?"

"Yes, the label was convinced that the world wanted us to be in love, and so we were told we needed to be in love. There wasn't really space for a conversation."

"And James didn't stop this? I mean, you've always talked about him like he is on your team."

I didn't mean to say what came out next. I had never told anyone this, not even Jess.

"That's the funny thing. It was *James's* idea. He pitched it to the label. I think he was under extra stress to make sure that this record did better than our last one. We hadn't done anything newsworthy recently, other than make music, and he thought this would stir the pot a little."

Saying that out loud made me feel like I was betraying James. But then, maybe he had betrayed me first.

6

January 20th

Eleanor

The release party for "Home" was a bizarre, out-of-body experience for Eleanor. The entire room was lit up like a dream. Eleanor reminded herself that she was getting everything she had ever dreamed of. She had a chart-topping song, for which she had the sole writing credit. This party was her celebration. The room was filled with her favorite people. She was with the guy the whole world believed was her one true love. From an outside perspective, Eleanor was the luckiest girl in the world.

So why did she feel so miserable?

If you saw snapshots of this night on the glossy pages of a shiny magazine, you might be jealous of Eleanor. Thousands of young women across America suddenly saw her as a threat, as if they had believed they had a chance of landing Art. You would have seen her draped in a flawless floor-length royal-blue sheath designed specifically for her, just for this night. You would have seen a new couple, madly in love, who were the stars of the show. Everything was perfect.

Eleanor, on the other hand, felt the wrongness of the moment keenly. Firstly, it felt awkward to suddenly be attending this party with a date. She had not mentally prepared for this situation. When you go to an event as a couple, you move from being an "I" to a "we." It no longer mattered how she felt about the song's release; it was all about what "we" felt. She couldn't go and talk to anyone she wished. According to James, she needed to be within her new boyfriend's line of sight to make their relationship more believable. Eleanor and Art were supposed to be newly living in the freedom of not having to keep their romance a secret anymore.

She was also wearing the blue dress. However beautiful and effortless it seemed; it pulled and pushed and tucked in all the wrong places in an attempt to make her look eight times smaller than she actually was. A straitjacket would have felt more comfortable. Not to mention the ensemble was paired with the tallest pair of stilettos she had worn in years. With every step, she was worried she would go crashing down.

At least she had someone's arm to lean on. Maybe she would be able to play this night off as romantic instead of clumsy.

For his part, Art was also not having the party that he envisioned. It had been a very awkward conversation when he called Korine that morning to un-invite her to the party. They had been planning for it to be their official first outing as a couple. On top of that disappointment, he had been told by James that he would no longer be allowed to see Korine, lest he is called the cheater, which would paint him in a terrible light and put the band at risk. He was under no circumstances to be caught "cheating" on Eleanor. It would be too much of a threat to the band. James reassured him that after their tour was over, he was welcome to call Korine again. But his tone implied that he doubted Art would even remember who Korine was nine months from now.

Art also had to explain to Korine that he was now dating Ellie. A lawyer would be by shortly with a non-disclosure agreement to sign, promising that she would not reveal any of their relationship's details under any circumstances. Their fling overlapped with the newly created Art and Ellie timeline. He was told that if he was asked about his relationship with Korine, he was to say that they were old friends. He was giving her career advice, as she was looking to get a start in music. This would be beneficial also for Korine, who was, in fact, thinking about branching out into the music industry. He hadn't denied the nature of his relationship with Korine because, at that point, his relationship with Eleanor was still a secret, and he hadn't wanted to risk exposing it.

Though the whole story had been well thought out, this did not make it more enjoyable for Art. Yes, he would admit that he had built a reputation as a player, but he didn't think this was a bad thing. He was young; this is what you were supposed to do while you were young. Plus, he was famous. It would be a waste of his talent not to play the field before settling down . . . if he ever chose to settle down at all.

It had been a silent ride to the party. Though Art and Ellie had never communicated much before, their silence now was slick with bitter anger. They each believed the other to be responsible for ruining their personal lives. Even if this was only for nine months or whatever James had said, it felt like life had been permanently turned upside down.

Ellie was already thinking of how they could break up in nine months without giving the impression they were breaking up the band. How do you break up a fake relationship?

Then, the idea hit her: this could finally be her chance to break away and have a solo career. That thought gave her a little hope. She could have agency over her music for once. She wouldn't have to share the stage with the selfish, narcissistic person whose arm was now linked with hers. This could be her ticket to freedom.

Maybe this was why James had agreed to this. Perhaps he saw this as the light at the end of the tunnel for Ellie. He could help her leave Kittanning. She could release a killer breakup album, and she would have the ability to control her music. The thought almost made her want to cry. That was the vision she needed to cling to if she were to survive this. She only needed to make it nine months, and then she would be free. Freer than she ever had imagined she could be.

On the other hand, Art had a different idea of what this new forced relationship could mean for his career. As Eleanor was planning a new life in the seat next to him, he considered how he could use this moment to remove her from the band. He had long suspected she had been plotting to steal the spotlight from him. What if their relationship got so serious that she had to quit? There was no way she could still tour if she were pregnant. Maybe she would sing back-up vocals on a song now and then, but she would have to retire, right? He could take back the band *and* be the good guy. It wouldn't be responsible for Eleanor to be a mom in a band. She would step down to tend to her motherly duties, and he would go out and continue making music. Honestly, it would leave them both looking great to the press. He couldn't deprive the world of his talent, could he?

They both believed their own plans were foolproof.

The evening was filled with flashing lights, and everyone begging for their attention. It all felt overwhelming to Eleanor. It wasn't that she hated doing interviews or having her picture taken. She and Art had not had any time together alone to process how they were going to handle these new situations. Even if this was a real relationship, they would have talked about and rehearsed who would stand on which side, who was going to be the straight man, and who would take the lead in answering questions. Eleanor was worried that if they fumbled through this awkwardly, it would affirm any doubts that this relationship was a fraud.

Thankfully, by the eighth time someone came over to gush at them, they had a semblance of a system.

Every time someone looked like they were coming over to talk to them about their newly announced love, Art would lean in a little closer as if he were going to tell her a secret. This way, it looked as if the person was interrupting an intimate moment between lovers. She found herself leaning into every word he said, no matter what he was talking about. She noticed herself laughing at all the right moments, gently touching his arm to show support and love. At the end of the evening, she realized that pretending with Art had not been as difficult as she had imagined.

Like any normal relationship, they had developed a go-to formulated response each time one of the typical relationship questions was asked.

Everyone knew how they met, so they didn't have to worry about coming up with a good "meet cute" story.

But everyone wanted to know how long they had been going out.

"Five months, but it feels like a lot longer because we have been best friends for so long!"

Eleanor had broken up with her last boyfriend six months ago, and James didn't want it to look like she might have cheated. Art had always refused to officially announce being in a relationship before this because he didn't want to be tied down. They didn't have to worry about a timeline matching his life.

After sorting out how long this had been going on, the person would say something along the lines of, "Wow, I had no idea—you guys hid it so well!"

They would laugh, and Eleanor would lean her head on Art's shoulder.

"We didn't want to spoil the magic," Art would say sweetly.

The next most-asked question was, "Who made the first move?"

The first time the question was asked, Art jumped to say, "I did. I watched her sing and saw her creative process. I realized that I was in love with her brain. I loved the way she thought and the way that she could turn any story into a song. And then, one day, we were working late on something at the studio, and I knew. I was in love with her. From that moment on, I knew that I would do whatever I could to show my love for her, and I only dreamed that one day she would love me too."

When Eleanor heard these words come out of his mouth, she had teared up. She had not believed him capable of such a beautiful compliment. These were the words Eleanor had always wanted to hear someone say. And here they were, spoken by someone she had so recently considered an enemy.

The interviewers tended to get teary as well, and then turn to Eleanor, "So when did you know that you loved him?"

The first time she was asked this, Eleanor was genuinely too shocked to have a decent answer. She didn't think that Art was capable of such a loving response, and she was genuinely thrown. Eleanor scrambled to regain some ground. She needed to make the world think that she was equally in love with him, or else when they broke up, she would be labeled as the bad guy.

She had never been quick at thinking on her feet.

"Well, I had always had a crush on Art. I mean, everyone does, come on. He is the world's nicest guy, and have you ever looked into his eyes?" She knew that this would feed his ego and was an opinion shared by many. Those piercing caramel eyes drew everyone in. All the girls she met wanted to date Art. "But it was just a crush . . . like I never actually thought that anything would happen. I didn't want to make a move and risk the band. And I didn't think that my heart would be able to handle an unrequited love. If I made a move, and he didn't like me back, I didn't think that I would be able to face him again. It is very vulnerable and scary to tell someone you spend so much time with that you like them. And what were the odds that he would actually like me back? Then, one night, it was us again alone in the studio. We spent a lot of time alone in the studio." She tried to look sly.

"Anyway, so one of those late nights, we were arguing back and forth over lyrics, which is something we do a lot. And we were going back and forth over this one line in "Done My Time," a song on the new album. There is a line that says, 'I can't spend one more sleepless night without you,' and Art looked over at me and said, 'Ellie, you deserve to be with the one you love,' and I just looked at him, and I knew. I had subconsciously written the song about him. The rest is history."

In reality, "Done My Time" had not been written about Art. She had written the song about her sister, Cora, with whom she had a broken relationship. But this was not something that she wanted to talk about. In a way, using Art as an excuse was the perfect way to keep the Band-Aid on, protecting that area of her personal life.

Finally, before turning to talk to someone else, their interrogator would almost always ask if they would be singing "Home" that night in celebration of its release. Everyone wanted to be there for the song's first live performance.

Truth be told, Art and Ellie had been entirely consumed with not ruining the first night of the fake relationship. Neither of them had thought that they would undoubtedly be asked to sing "Home."

Halfway through the night, they were approached by James.

"Everyone is asking when you two are going to sing. You have to sing the song tonight. I know that you haven't practiced together, but you have been singing together for so long, what could go wrong?"

A lot could go wrong, both Eleanor and Art thought simultaneously. However, neither one wanted to be the first to admit this, especially not at the song's release party, especially not to James.

"James, do we even have the sound equipment here?" Eleanor asked cautiously. This was a roundabout way to admit that she didn't want to have to sing tonight. She had drunk just enough to be worried about making a fool of herself.

James smiled grimly. "Funny you should ask. The venue has basic mics, and I have the track music from the song. You just need to sing along. I am sure that everyone will find it really spontaneous and spur of the moment. It is just the kind of thing two people madly in love would do."

This whole day had felt spontaneous, thought Eleanor. She was starting to wonder how well-planned all this spontaneity had been.

"Fine." Art said finally. "But this is not going to be a big thing. Tell people to put their phones away—make it seem top secret. It will add to the allure of it. And we will make sure to tell them that it was not planned, in case something goes wrong."

James agreed.

Forty-five minutes later, Eleanor and Art were sharing a stage for the first time as a couple. Jenny and Chip were told they were not needed. It felt awkward and lonely without them.

All in all, their first performance could have gone a lot worse. They both attempted to lean into the fact that they were a couple more than they should have. Trying to share a microphone is not as romantic as one might guess. But they fumbled through it. No matter how awkward the whole thing felt to Kittanning, the rest of the crowd seemed overjoyed to have been in the room where it happened. They had gotten to see a little piece of history, and that was enough to let them quickly overlook any onstage awkwardness.

"That was perfect!" James exploded when they got off the stage. "This was the best move we ever could have made for the band," he whispered quietly into their ears as he pulled them into an embrace.

The band followed their tradition of all piling into one car to debrief their evening.

"Never in my life have I been asked more questions about you," Jenny sighed as soon as the door to the car was shut. "I don't know if I am frustrated that people seemed to have forgotten every song needs a drummer or honored that I was spoken to so much."

"I am sorry you had to deal with that, Jenny," Eleanor said sympathetically. It was one of her greatest fears that her friend would feel overlooked.

"I should have expected it. I honestly didn't think that so many people would actually care whether or not I had known all along that you two would end up together."

"End up together, ugh," Art said, mimicking vomiting. "I love how this has been news for ten hours, and our wedding is already planned."

"Well, less work for you," added Chip. "Planning a wedding is lots more work than you could ever imagine."

"So, what did you say?" Eleanor turned to Jenny.

"I said the only thing I could think of without giving away too many details. I said, 'I was never really sure, but I was always rooting for you two.'"

Her comment was met with silence.

Eleanor knew that this was a lie. She knew that Jenny had never wanted them to date, not just because she was afraid of the group being the next ABBA. There was a girl code about this sort of thing: an unspoken knowledge that Eleanor would never date Art because he was not the right guy. She was sure that she would receive a cryptic text from Jenny that night saying that she loved and supported her, no matter what. Eleanor knew that Jenny would never come out and say it, for fear of ruining the band, but she would support Eleanor in the words she left unsaid.

Chip was sure his wife did not want Eleanor and Art together, and he knew that they would be having a separate debrief as soon as they got home. If she had wished to match Ellie and Art, she would have done so. Jenny loved playing cupid. She was the one who had set Eleanor up with her last boyfriend. If she had had a master plan for Eleanor and Art to be together, he would have known about it, and they would already have been together.

Art took this comment as a sign that Jenny was on his side. He had never known how to feel about Jenny. She was somewhat invasive, and, in fact, Art was surprised that she had not already tried to set him and Eleanor up. Maybe she figured that he would never take the bait. However, if Jenny had actually always been rooting for them as a couple, he wanted her on his side. Her support would be crucial when the time came for Eleanor to settle down and leave the band.

James wasn't even listening to the conversation; he was just basking in the relief that they had made it through the evening without a major hiccup.

7

August 31st

Cynthia

I wasn't entirely sure what I was supposed to wear on my first day of school. Many girls consulted friends on this, seeing it as a significant choice that took weeks or months. I, on the other hand, was lost and confused.

Also, as an adult, I felt like I should have had this all figured out.

Trying to sound casual, I asked: "Hey, so what should I wear tomorrow?" We were spending our Sunday afternoon reading inside. Kristy, it would seem, was the master of a casual Sunday.

"I have a feeling you are not going to like the answer," she replied grimly. "Do you see this?" she said, motioning to her pajamas. "This is what some people wear to class. I mean, some people dress up. Still, if you want to fit in and avoid drawing attention to yourself, I'd suggest a pair of running shorts and an old sweatshirt."

"Running shorts and an old sweatshirt? First, ew. Second, I don't have either of those."

"You're in luck," she told me with a grin. "That's like the weekend wardrobe of everyone in Seattle."

·◦~ᘏ◦;◦ᕟ~◦·

The next morning, I couldn't help but feel very underdressed.

Randy didn't comment on my attire when I got into his car, which I figured was a good sign. If I had been wrongly dressed, I trusted that he would have at least given me a funny look.

I didn't know what I was supposed to say on the car ride to campus. Was I supposed to give some sort of explanation of why I had randomly decided to start university, including why I had decided to do it with a bodyguard?

"So, is this a 'The Prince and Me' situation?" Randy asked after a few blocks. He flashed a smile at me in the rearview mirror.

I had to choke back a laugh, spilling the coffee I was holding in my hand.

"Are you asking me if I am secretly royalty? Do you really think royalty would dress like this?" I said, mentioning Kristy's old sweatshirt, now complete with a newly stained sleeve.

"You look like a college student. If you were royalty, you would have done some research on how to blend in."

"Okay, good, so this is what a college student actually wears. I had a panic this morning that Kristy was playing a weird practical joke on me."

Randy smiled reassuringly, "Don't worry, you will blend right in, Your Majesty."

"Perfect."

"Definitely a good thing you left the tiara at home, though; that would have been a dead giveaway."

"Oh, really? Shame, I had read in 'Princesses Weekly' that casual tiara-wearing was going to make a comeback this year."

"You never know, it might. You could be that trendsetter."

"They really are a practical accessory. More people should wear them."

"I think wars have been fought on the other side of your argument."

I laughed, put at ease by the lighthearted banter. "Maybe I will learn about it in school today!"

As I stepped out of the car onto the college campus, I felt a little burst of hope.

"Okay, this is it," I said, taking a deep breath. "Meet back here after class?"

"Yep, I will be the guy creepily following you."

"Great, loving this plan."

I really felt like I had an extra pep in my step.

It lasted until I reached the classroom, where I was met with another issue. Where was I supposed to sit?

The room was a lot larger than I thought, and I realized that I needed to be in a spot where Randy could see me but not too close to him to blow our cover.

I picked a seat on the aisle and started to pull out my notebook. I wasn't really sure what I would need on the first day of class. Riffling through my backpack full of notebooks, I was beginning to think I might have over-packed.

"I'm sorry, but are you left-handed?" a baritone voice inquired behind me.

I could tell this was about to be the weirdest pick-up line I had ever heard.

"Sorry, I'm not giving autographs," I said the words before I even realized they were out. It was a second-nature response. The words came out as easy as breathing.

"Dude, I don't want your autograph. I wanted to know if you are sitting at a left-handed desk because you are left-handed."

I suddenly realized my mistake. The aisle seats on this side of the room all had their desks on the other side of the chair so that left-handed people could write easier.

I could hear Randy muffle a laugh from a few rows back.

"Oh gosh, I'm sorry. It's my first day of class, and I am still getting the hang of this. No, I am not left-handed. I'm sorry," I repeated, moving over a chair. "It's all yours!" I tapped the seat, indicating for him to sit down.

Who does that? Who taps a seat inviting someone to sit down? Old women telling their grandchildren where to sit and creepy men trying to seduce a woman in a '90s movie. I could feel my face redden with embarrassment. It didn't help that my new classmate was nerdy cute, with the classic square glasses and sweater-over-button-down combination. Under the nerd uniform, though, he bore a remarkable resemblance to Adam Scott.

"Sweet, thanks." He plopped down into the chair, flashing me a broad smile. "Thanks for warming it up for me."

Oh, my gosh. Do I have a warm butt? Have I always been such an awkward person and just had the privilege of living behind the mask of fame that conveniently hid my awkwardness?

"By the way, I'm Gabe. Welcome to Seattle U."

"Hi, thanks." I tried to act normal. Gabe looked like someone's favorite brother, and he was dressed as if he could, at any moment, produce a pen and notepad. Eleanor thought he reminded her of that charming, unassuming guy the label always sent to deliver bad news: too friendly and cute to warrant a negative reaction.

"Uh, what's your name?"

"Oh, sorry, duh. I'm Cynthia."

"Where are you from, Cynthia?"

I panicked. Where was I from?

"I grew up outside of Pittsburgh."

"So, are you new to Seattle?"

"Yeah."

"Well, good luck this fall. If people hear you are from Pittsburgh, Seattle can be a dangerous place."

I started to panic; my hands were sweating uncontrollably. Was I usually this sweaty?

"Oh gosh, why?"

"Are you a sports fan?"

"Oh, duh," the answer hit me; I knew this! "The 2006 Super Bowl?"

"Yeah, people around here are not over it."

"What's to be over?" I teased, "The Seahawks lost, fair and square! The team with the most points when the clock hits zero wins, right?"

"You *know* the ref was bribed!"

"There is no evidence of that," I countered.

"He retired after that game!"

"He had a long career; it was time to hang up his whistle!"

"Man, I thought this was going to be a long-lasting friendship here, Cynthia. But I don't think I can sit by you tomorrow. First, you take my desk, which come on, you have to give the leftie a break, the desks are discriminatory. Then you come into my city and tell me that the Hawks weren't denied their Super Bowl?"

"It's a dog-eat-dog world."

"Fair point. So, tell me, why did you move to Seattle? Obviously not because of a deep love of Seattle sports teams."

I had to play this off as a joke; I hadn't expected a "why did you move here" question so quickly.

"I thought you said that there was no hope of a friendship. That's a very friend-like question."

"You're right, I take it back."

"Good." I couldn't help but smile.

College was starting to feel like an excellent idea.

"I saw you made a friend," Randy said as soon as we were both in the car.

"Yeah, yeah, yeah," I said, rolling my eyes. "He's a Hawks fan, so the friendship can only go so far."

"Oh no, do you like the Niners?"

"I'm from Pittsburgh, so you fill in the blank."

"Oh, a Steelers fan, you have *got* to be kidding me. If you weren't paying me so well, I would kindly let you out of the car here."

"Yeah, yeah yeah," I repeated.

I had bought a bottle of wine and ordered some Thai food to celebrate my successful first day. It felt like this insane plan was actually going to work.

My euphoria lasted until Kristy got home. I was all set to greet her with a wine glass and a dish of gossip. However, I started to panic as soon as she walked through the door. She looked anxious, almost distraught.

"Did you get on Twitter today?" She was out of breath by the time she walked through the door.

"No, not today." I had been making a point to avoid social media. I didn't want to accidentally make some stupid mistake and reveal where I was. I guess I could create a burner account. Most people had them; I just hadn't felt the need to yet. It was nice not to be connected all of the time.

"It got leaked. Someone leaked that you are gone."

"Wait, what?" The bubble I had been floating around in all day suddenly popped.

"I don't know—someone leaked that you weren't touring anymore, that no one has seen you since the concert."

"Did the band make a comment?" My hands were suddenly even sweatier than they had been in class earlier.

"Yes, their official statement is that you have stopped touring for personal reasons, whatever that is supposed to mean."

"Oh my gosh, that makes it sound like I am in rehab or like I had a mental breakdown."

"I mean, it sure doesn't make it sound good."

"Did it mention the engagement?"

Kristy's face reddened.

"What?" I demanded.

"Everything refers to him as your fiancé."

"Okay, that much I expected. Has Art said anything?"

"The last post on his Instagram feed is a picture taken from the show in Denver to announce your engagement."

"Wait, what?" This I had not seen; I hadn't checked any social media since that show. It hadn't occurred to me that he would probably post about it.

"Well, to be honest, it is a charming picture. If I didn't know everything that was going on, I'd say it was the dream engagement."

I hated to admit it, but she was right. I had thought about this a lot. If anyone else I knew had their boyfriend propose to them in the same way Art had proposed to me, I would have been elated. It had been adorable and well thought out, and there were guaranteed to be loads of good pictures of the ask. And, honestly, it had been the most romantic setting imaginable to me: the place I love—the stage—with the people I love—our fans.

But every love story has layers. My story felt more like an onion.

"Can I see the picture?" I wasn't sure if this was a brave or a stupid request.

Kristy grabbed her phone and pulled up his page.

A concert to remember, Denver. We love you even more now! The picture was captioned, posted the morning after the show—the morning after I left for good.

"*We?*" That was all I could say. He had lumped me into this. He and I had become we. Little did the world know, I hadn't said one word to him since that night.

The picture was incredible; there was no way to deny that. It had been taken from a slightly different angle than the one on the magazine. This one felt a little more intimate. It had clearly been staged; the camera was focused on our faces. We were on center stage, a chorus of people behind us, Chip and Jenny to our left. Even though the picture was zoomed out, it was easy to tell I was crying. My hands were partway over my mouth. I did look shocked. He was on one knee; his eyes looked full of hope.

It didn't look like he was faking the whole thing at all. He looked like he really loved me. I just looked shocked.

In his defense, I had not said no. There really had not been another choice. What was I supposed to do in a stadium full of people? It had been a very strategic move on his part. In theory, he had every right to refer to us as "we." But he couldn't have thought I had actually agreed to marry him. Especially after disappearing. Especially after leaving his grandmother's ring in my dressing room. Right?

"Okay, this is not as bad as I thought it might be. In some ways, it is a relief to have people know I am no longer on the road. It will make it quicker for people to forget about me and move on. And I mean, it was going to come out sometime. I am surprised it came out so soon, but we are on tour. I don't know what I was expecting; there are always more eyes on you during a tour."

It wasn't as bad as I thought it was going to be. I was sure that there would be a video or picture of him out with another girl released soon. The world would accuse him of cheating, and he would no longer be the perfect boyfriend who planned the most romantic proposal. He would be a cheater. And maybe then the world would side with me, and I could come out of hiding. I could have my career back.

I missed the music. I had been gone for not even two weeks, and I missed it desperately. I missed talking about it; I missed planning shows; I missed writing songs . . . I missed the whole thing. If I waited this out, I might actually be able to have the career I had always dreamed of. That dream was worth hanging on to.

"Well, there is a little more you need to know." Kristy's face reddened slightly more.

"Yes?" I said nervously.

"So, he is going to give an interview on the *Morning Show* this week."

"Just him or the whole band?"

"I mean, from what I read, I think that it's just him."

"Like to talk about what, our love, and how he wants the world to rally around me as I go through this difficult time?"

"Honestly, that would probably be a good PR move for him, right?"

I hated that my life had become a question of what the better PR move was. But Kristy was probably right. It would make him look like a fantastic guy, a supportive fiancé—every girl's dream.

"Are you going to watch it?"

"I feel like I should . . . just to see what he has to say about the whole thing. I don't want to be blindsided." I winced.

"I tell you what. I'll go in late to work so I can watch it with you."

"Thank you," I said weakly.

I had no idea what to expect. All I knew was I felt sick to my stomach.

February 8th

Eleanor

The weeks leading up to the release of an album are always a little crazy. A newly formed fake relationship added just one more thing to try to manage.

Eleanor was able to find a makeshift system. She found another apartment to rent in Art's building through Jess's manager. James didn't even know she had done this. It was top secret. If she had to suffer through this nightmare of a relationship, she would at least have a place where she could feel a little bit of peace. Just the idea of staying in Art's apartment made her feel unsafe.

Three nights a week, Eleanor and Art went out to dinner, as per their agreement with James. Then, they would go back to Art's place. At least that's what it looked like.

Some nights, she would go into his apartment. He was not a terrible conversationalist. On nights they didn't finish a conversation at dinner, she would go back to his apartment, have a drink, and talk. It was nice. For the first time since the band had gotten together, Art felt like a friend, someone she could actually talk to. It was a welcome change of pace. They fell into a comfortable rhythm, and Eleanor began to let down her guard.

Then, one night they had been discussing the anti-trust laws surrounding draft regulations in pro sports. Eleanor had spent a lot of time researching the topic—it was one of her nerdy passions that she rarely got the chance to talk about.

Art and Eleanor were both big Steelers fans (as were Chip and Jenny, of course). When you grow up in western Pennsylvania, it's in your blood. They talked about the upcoming season and coaching changes. Eleanor liked college football more than pro, which was why she found the draft laws fascinating. Still, she was happy to talk about either.

It was refreshing to be aligned with Art on something. It was nice to hear his opinion on things away from a camera. She liked that he would share his thoughts freely without fearing that he would make a wrong step.

They had less than a week before the album was released. Both Art and Eleanor were feeling a tired excitement that only comes around an album release.

He had invited her to come in.

She liked talking about sports, so she had.

In her mind, her apartment was just down the hall; she would just go home in an hour. She had done this before. It was becoming a sort of tradition.

But this time felt different.

Eleanor walked into his apartment, just like she had many times in the past weeks.

Something was off.

She tried to remember if Art had drunk more than usual. Maybe he had.

Something was different.

She tentatively closed the door behind her, trying to ignore her heart beating fast in her throat.

"So, we're doing this," Art said as soon as she closed the door.

He *was* different. His speech was rougher, and he swayed a little as he stepped closer.

"What do you mean?" Eleanor felt off-balance, confused about how he had concluded that she would be spending the night.

"Ellie, come on, I know you are into me. I mean, if we are going to have to do all the work of this relationship thing, we might as well get some of the rewards." He winked. Her stomach turned.

"Art, I am not into you, not like that."

"Come on," he huffed, "no girl wants to spend an hour debating draft rules."

"I do." She tried to catch his eyes, show him she was sincere, but he wasn't looking at her eyes.

"Yeah, right," he said, taking another step closer.

"Art, this is not happening."

He towered over her. "Ellie, let's be real. I know that you have wanted to sleep with me for years now."

"No." It was the only word that she could get out of her mouth

He lunged for her.

She lunged for the door, but he caught her tightly by the arm, his fingers pressing painfully into her skin.

"Come on, Ellie." He moved his hand to her cheek, possessively. "You need to just get over yourself. You are not as talented as you think; you might as well do something to help yourself get ahead." He sneered, "You would be *nothing* without me. You think that just because . . ."

Ellie tore herself from his grasp, pried open the door, and slammed it before he could finish his sentence.

She went to open the door to her apartment when she realized that she had left her phone and keys behind. Her body shook with angry sobs. There was no way that she was going back there tonight.

Instead, she went down to the doorman.

On her way to the lobby, Eleanor calmed herself down and dabbed the running mascara off her face. She didn't want to give the doorman a reason to believe that something was wrong.

She mustered a polite smile. "I'm so sorry, but I seem to have locked my keys in my apartment. Could you please help me out?"

"Sure thing, doll, I'll be up there in a minute."

Once the doorman was gone, she had a sickening realization. Because her keys were in Art's apartment, he could technically let himself in if he wanted. Her keys were in her purse on the table next to his front door. She prayed that he wouldn't even notice her small black bag.

Just to be safe, she moved all the furniture she could in front of the door. She didn't want to take any chances.

The next morning, she regained some of her courage, although she had not slept at all. She was too rattled by the night before to calm her mind.

Art had a very different perspective on the previous night's events.

After Ellie left his apartment, he had gone into a rage. How could she possibly get away with treating him like that?

In his anger, he had broken a vase with flowers that someone had sent him. Since announcing his relationship with Eleanor, many companies had been sending him "congratulations" bouquets that came in fancy vases. His apartment was now full of the stupid things.

How could she be so dumb? He knew that she was selfish, but he didn't think she was that stupid. Didn't she understand what he was doing for her by being in this silly relationship? It was only because of him that anyone knew—let alone cared—about Eleanor Quinn. He had made her who she was. He deserved at least a little respect from her.

And, on top of it, why would she have spent the night talking about sports unless she wanted to sleep with him? She had purposefully led him on, just to storm out on him.

What a tease.

He had bigger things to worry about, including an album coming out next week. He would not let one stupid woman knock him off his game. That was probably exactly what she wanted. In fact, this was probably all part of her foolish plan. Seduce him and then leave him hanging . . . bait him into doing something stupid to mess up his career. She was so manipulative. Did she really think he would fall for that? Art was smart. He would outwit her. Instead of sleeping, Art spent the rest of his night plotting and planning.

9

September 2nd

Cynthia

Sleep was escaping me. I hadn't become an insomniac, per se, but this had been happening more and more frequently. I'd have hours where I would just lie in bed, awake.

This was a new problem for me. I used to brag about how well I could sleep: on tour buses as well as in my own bed. Others would roll their eyes and tell me to consider myself lucky; sleep is a precious commodity. I didn't realize how prized good rest was until I didn't have it anymore. Nights like this made me want to cry.

I knew exactly why I wasn't able to sleep. I could *not* stop thinking about Art's interview. I found myself obsessing over what I thought he might say. Honestly, he was so unpredictable that anything could come out of his mouth.

I knew enough to know that I didn't trust him as far as I could throw him. He'd try to pull something.

I rolled over and looked at the clock, even though seeing the time was never helpful. As a kid, I would start to cry if I couldn't fall asleep by 10:00 p.m. I had this deep-rooted anxiety that I was never going to sleep again. I punched my pillow and rolled over to stare at the ceiling.

It was almost 3:00 a.m. Art was probably heading to the studio now. His interview was going to be at 9:00 Eastern, which meant 6:00 a.m. in Seattle.

My inability to sleep through the night was a post-Art phenomenon. I could sleep just fine until we started "dating."

The guilt crawled in. How could I have let this happen? I could feel the spiral of thoughts taking over, keeping me awake.

This was my fault.

What if he had meant it when he told me that he loved me? What if the way he acted was just how love is supposed to be?

But then I thought of all the things he had said to me. The marks I had found on my upper arm the morning after I escaped his apartment.

How could I have let myself be treated like this?

He had told me one night that I would never amount to anything, especially without him. What if he was right?

I didn't believe him. But a small, shaky part of me still wondered.

The whole thing felt even more confusing at three in the morning.

My mind circled back to the interview. There was a good chance that he would spend the whole time talking about himself. That would be a very Art thing to do. He could use my "break for personal reasons" to imply how great a guy he was and cause the world to fall even more in love with him. He'd probably just mention my mental state in passing. Just enough to get pity but not enough to make *me* the center of *his* interview. Art would quickly move on to talking about something he was working on.

I chanced a glance at the clock. 4:01 a.m. I would only have to wait two more hours to find out.

I sighed, grabbed Kristy's old sweatshirt, and stumbled through the dark to the kitchen. Four o'clock wasn't too early to start the day, I tried to justify to myself. Commuters and stock-brokers did this all the time! Plus, Kristy was a deep sleeper. She always bragged that nothing woke her up at night.

I would never call myself a baker, but I had become one, thanks to all the sleepless nights. Since moving to Kristy's, I had become an expert middle-of-the-night baker. Tonight, I decided that I was going to make banana bread. It would be an ideal breakfast.

Baking was the perfect way to take my mind off my current problems. It required me to think and measure and calculate. And, as a bonus, my labor almost always led to something delicious.

I thumped down my measuring cup, flour spilling itself across the countertop.

This was my problem. *This* was what I was afraid was going to happen with Art. I had measured and calculated the relationship and the control I thought I had over the narrative. I had believed I would be able to end it without hurting the band or myself in the process.

But somewhere along the line, the plan had gotten messed up. Something was incorrectly measured. This was not how I had pictured it would be. The result was a mess.

This was why I preferred baking. I was in control the whole time; I could better handle all the variables. My flour was not going to decide that it didn't feel like making a cake and march off and do its own thing.

I just needed to be able to control the outcome of something and not mess it up.

·ᴄᴏ᠔ᵒᠻᴄ᠍ᴏᵒᵗ·

Around 5:30, Kristy stumbled out of her room. I greeted her with a cup of coffee.

"Did you sleep at all?" she asked with a tone of concern.

"Believe me, I tried. Instead, we have banana bread."

I could tell that she was doing her best to hide her sympathetic look.

"You know I have been craving banana bread for weeks, and I just haven't gotten around to making it yet."

"I am 80 percent sure you are lying. But thank you."

"So, how do you want to do this? Do you want to watch this together? Do you want me to make you an Irish coffee? Should I grab some paper so we can crumple it and throw it at the TV? What's our move?"

"Well, what did you do the last time that your fake ex-fiancé addressed your fans on national TV?"

"I'll grab the paper and a box of tissues."

·ᴄᴏ᠔ᵒᠻᴄ᠍ᴏᵒᵗ·

Twenty minutes later, we had settled on the couch. I couldn't stop shaking. I had to fight the urge to get up and pace the room.

I felt angry and stressed. This was the first time a band member had made a solo TV show appearance. I hadn't even been briefed beforehand.

It felt like I was on the edge of a cliff and forced to jump without knowing how far of a drop it was.

The opening credits came on, and an overly cheery face greeted America. I felt like I was going to puke. I was most definitely going to puke. How in the world was I going to survive this? Part of me wanted to run to my room and just wait to get a debriefing from Kristy afterward.

But no. I was not going to let Art ruin my day, ruin my life.

"Are you sure you want to do this?" Kristy asked me as the first commercial break came on. They had just announced that he would be interviewed after the break.

"I have to do this. I need to know what he is going to say about me."

She squeezed my hand.

The commercial ended. "And we are back, with Art Bishop, lead singer of America's favorite band, Kittanning. Good morning, Art!"

"Good morning, Cheryl," he said to the interviewer. It was so weird seeing him like this. I had seen him give many interviews, but Jenny, Chip, and I had always been there. It was odd seeing him in the spotlight alone.

"What a year it has been for you! First, congratulations on your new album being the most-streamed pop album this year. You guys have been playing a sold-out tour. At a recent show, you melted America's heart with the proposal that every woman in America could only dream of. How has this year felt for you? Has it felt as magical for you as it has from our point of view?"

What a leading question. I was sure that Art had set this up. He was probably looking for pity. Ugh. I wadded up a piece of paper and hurled it at the TV.

Kristy arched an eyebrow. "Wow, already? He's barely said two words! I'm not judging," she reassured me with a laugh, "but maybe I should have grabbed more paper."

Art responded, "It has been a crazy year, Cheryl. When you list it in one sentence, it's hard to believe all that happened just this year." He flashed a brilliant smile. Ah, his interview personality sure was laying it on thick today, making me nervous for what was coming next. "But what you said is right. It's easy to hear this year's events and think that I am living a fantasy, but, sadly, that has really not been the case. Honestly, this month, I'm just barely holding it together."

Cheryl, skilled interviewer that she was, nodded as if to encourage him to say more. I knew him well enough to know he would wait until she asked another question before he spoke again. He told me once that he didn't want to give it all away on the first question. You had to leave them wanting more.

"Wow, can you fill us in on what has been going on behind the scenes?" Cheryl asked, captivated. At this, Art teared up. I wondered what type of acting coach he had hired to master those fake tears. Never in my life had I ever seen Art Bishop cry. I fired more paper at the TV.

Cheryl was falling for it. She handed him a box of tissues, pity etched on her face. He took one, turning away from the camera to wipe his eyes.

"Thank you," he said, blowing out a sigh and shaking his head. "It's just been really hard, and this will be the first time I share our story publicly."

"Take your time and thank you for being willing to share your story."

The nauseous feeling in my stomach increased; whatever he was about to say was undoubtedly designed to make me look bad.

Art looked straight at the camera, "I want to start by clarifying that I love my band and my bandmates. They have made me who I am today, and I respect them all deeply. Earlier this year, Eleanor Quinn and I went public with our relationship. It seemed like the most logical thing to do. We are in love, and we wanted the world to know about it."

I sighed in relief. Art wasn't going to tell all of America that our relationship had been a lie. That was probably a good thing. However, I couldn't help but notice he was still talking about our love in the present tense. I didn't know if his continuation of the lie made me feel better or worse. I did know that this meant he would expect me to keep up the charade.

"I have known Eleanor for all of my life," Art explained to Cheryl. "We grew up on the same street; our parents see each other at the grocery store. Even putting aside the band, we did not take the decision to start dating lightly. Our lives have always been so intertwined."

I thought of Jenny as he made this comment. It felt like he was trying to reassure her.

"But, like I said, we just knew that what we have is different, and with all of my heart, I love Eleanor." Art looked straight at me, "I want to marry her."

Even though he was looking at a camera in a studio, I knew his words were aimed straight at me. Not because he loved me. He was threatening me with marriage if I reappeared and told the truth.

Art continued, "Nobody knows Eleanor as well as I do."

"Liar!" Kristy yelled, lobbing her own ball of paper at his smug face. I imagined that if Jess were watching, she would be having a similar reaction.

"And I have known for a while now that she was struggling with some mental health issues. She has needed help for years. I mean, we've all seen a shrink off and on; that's normal. But for Ellie, it ran deeper. I started to get really worried; I mean, the whole band was worried."

At this, the camera panned to the crowd, where Jenny and Chip were sitting in the front row with teary eyes, holding hands. They looked like I had died, and this was my funeral.

"She started cutting off members of her family, like her sister, who didn't even know we were dating until we announced it to the press. She called me, really hurt. She didn't know why Eleanor hadn't called her. Cora, her sister, was worried that her secret-keeping was the root of another issue. Sadly, now, I am afraid she was right. Again, I've known her whole family forever, so it's not weird for me to talk to her sister. I've known her just as long as I've known Ellie."

At this, both Kristy and I threw paper at the screen.

Kristy paused the TV.

"Of course, Cora's riding on the tailwinds of this. This is just like her." I spat the words out before Kristy could say anything else. "She doesn't talk to me. *That* is why she didn't know about the relationship. *And* Art knows about my issues with my sister, and he's manipulating the situation to make me look terrible."

"Of course, Cora wouldn't have known that you and Art were dating; it was a fake relationship! You barely had time to call your own mother before the press was all over this!"

"Also, what is Art even doing talking to her in the first place?" I huffed. "He knows I'm watching and is just trying to tick me off. Maybe he's trying to pressure me into doing something stupid. Maybe he's just trying to make me jealous in his twisted way. Ugh!" I collapsed back in my seat, exhausted.

"Ready for me to play again?" Kristy motioned to the TV.

"Yes, let's get this over with."

"Tour has always been a difficult thing for Ellie, and this tour was no exception. If anything, there was almost more pressure than normal, given the success of the album. One night, it got to the point where she came to me saying that she wasn't sure she would be able to do this for much longer. Of course, at the time, I had no idea what she meant. We've all faced some tour fatigue. Everyone gets burnt out by their jobs at times. At first, I thought that was what she meant. But, over time, I realized this was different. She wouldn't let it drop, and, I will never forget this . . . she looked at me that night and said, 'I think this is my last tour.'"

I am not sure whose gasp was louder, mine, Kristy's, or Cheryl's.

"Wow! That is unexpected, coming from her. I always thought that Eleanor Quinn lived for the stage!"

"She was really good at showing people the side of her they wanted to see. She didn't think she would be seen as successful if she told people how hard touring actually was for her. So, I was thinking, what was something I could do to bring joy back to performing? That was when I had the proposal idea."

"Now *I* am going to need those tissues," Cheryl fake sniffed. "Knowing your motivation makes an adorable proposal even cuter! Tell me more about that."

Art blushed as if he was still smitten by the whole thing.

"I might need another tissue, too. I can still barely get through the story without tearing up; I can't believe it actually happened. I feel like the luckiest guy in the world."

"Gag me," I said. His fans were going to eat this interview up; this was the soft and sensitive side of Art they had always been dying to see.

"I knew that we were going to play this show in Denver, one more show, and then a week-long break. My initial plan had been to use that week-long break to go somewhere to celebrate. Ellie didn't know this, but I had booked tickets to Lisbon. It's her favorite city, and the last time we were there on tour, she didn't get to spend much time there. I thought if I proposed in Denver, it would take her mind off of everything until the next show. A vacation was supposed to help strengthen her for the remainder of the tour. That was my plan, at least. I talked to the band, and we slightly altered the setlist for that night. They were so supportive of the whole thing; they were willing to do whatever it took to give Ellie the perfect proposal. We all knew how difficult this year and this tour had been on her."

He paused dramatically.

"I had spent months planning the perfect proposal. At our shows, we cover a famous artist from each town we visit. One of Ellie's favorite songs is 'Ho, Hey,' by The Lumineers, from Colorado. She knew that we were planning on covering that song, but she had no idea that I had actually worked it out to bring The Lumineers there. We'd do a piano solo. Chip had been saying for a while that he wished he could play the piano more live. Jenny joined him on the banjo." He gave a tragic smile. "She learned how to play just for this song."

That was a lie. Jenny had known how to play the banjo for ages; she just didn't have many opportunities to play the banjo in a pop band. And Chip never got to showcase his outstanding piano skills because Art hogged the spotlight.

"During what she thought was going to be the piano solo was when I made my speech. She was stunned. You saw the pictures; it was perfect. I was on Cloud Nine. I had wrapped her in a hug, and I will never forget she whispered, 'I don't think I can sing any more tonight.' She was laughing and crying. It was precious. I told her not to worry about it, and the Lumineers went ahead and finished the song. She even managed to finish the set. We had, I think, two songs after that, and then the encore. It was something else. She sang with more joy than I had ever seen. Our last song before the encore was 'Done My Time.' I had never heard her sing more beautifully. It felt like she was singing straight to my soul. As if the song was for me. As if she knew that now she would never have to be without me again. Cheryl, even with everything else that followed, it was the best night of my life."

I'm sure it was. It was the night you got rid of me, I thought to myself.

"Wow, it sounds even more like a fairytale when you tell the story. I don't think there is a dry eye in the studio this morning. How romantic! So, what happened next? This is the part of the story the world didn't get to see, am I correct?"

"Yes. The next part of the story is something that only my bandmates have heard. I mean, we've all been living with it. Like I said earlier, Eleanor had some mental health issues that hadn't been resolved. It was obvious to us all, to anyone who knows her, really. We have a post-show tradition to share a beer brewed in the city we just played. That's how we actually rate playing in different cities," he said with a sly smile.

"We were all drinking our beer. Eleanor was sitting on my lap, admiring her ring—it had been my grandmother's diamond. I could tell she was happy. But something felt off. When I asked her if she was okay, she said 'yes, just tired.' She excused herself to the bathroom, a few minutes went by, and she hadn't come back." Art's face was grim.

"Jenny went and checked her dressing room, and she noticed that it was in slight disarray. As if she had been looking for something. There wasn't a note or anything. Her wallet was gone, and she hadn't changed her clothes because her costume wasn't there. I don't think any of us believed she was gone until, a few hours later, James got a text from her saying that she was okay."

Kristy paused the TV again. "Sorry, I have so many questions, and I want to ask them now before I forget. First, do you still have his ring?"

"No, and I think that's the real reason they knew I was gone. I left the ring on the dresser in my dressing room. I didn't want him to think I was buying into his fake engagement. I didn't want the ring to be a reason for him to come after me. Like, if it *was* his grandmother's ring, which he had told me that night it was, I didn't want to run off with it."

"Smart. Okay, second, is 'Ho Hey' seriously your favorite song? It's so old!"

"That's your burning question?! I mean, yes, it was, until two weeks ago."

"Okay, that's all I got for now. Are you okay?"

I took a deep breath, "Yes, I think so."

"Play on!"

Cheryl's eyes widened, "Wow. And you guys had to leave pretty quickly to be able to make it to the next stop on your tour?"

"Yes, and James had sent a jet for her, offering, no questions asked, to pick her up wherever she was so she could make it to the next show in time. He tried to appeal to the fact that she still loved me, and she still loved the band, but she was too far gone at that point. It has been two weeks now, and I haven't heard anything from her." Art hung his head. "She is the woman I love, and I don't even know how to reach her. She's mentally unstable, and I want to do all that I can to get her the help she needs. We had already discussed it and decided that she would step down from the band after this tour, but I had not imagined it would be like this."

"Wait, are you saying that she was going to leave the band?" Cheryl seemed shocked.

"Yes. We both made the decision that her health is the priority. We planned for me to stay in the band, and she would help with some writing when she felt up to it. But, after this incident, I feel really unsure about everything. I know she will want me to keep touring and making music because she knows how much it means to me and the world. But for her, the best choice was to stop permanently."

Paper wads and a box of tissues went hurling toward the TV.

"What does this mean for you, for your relationship? The whole country is rooting for you, especially now, knowing what you have had to deal with." Cheryl put her hand on his arm as if to comfort him.

"That is a tough question. I honestly thought that I would have heard from Ellie by now. We normally talk non-stop. I keep checking my phone, waiting to see her face light up the screen."

He pulled out his phone as if to demonstrate what he meant. His background was conveniently a picture of his proposal.

"So, you're saying you haven't heard from her at all?"

He took a long breath. Wow, I seriously needed to hire his acting coach.

"Cheryl, not only have I not heard from her, but it breaks my heart to tell you that I have no idea where she is. That's why it was so important for me to give this interview today. I miss my fiancée. I love her—more than I can put into words. But I know she is unstable. I have no idea where she is. I don't believe that she is at risk of harming herself or others, but I have no idea what her mental state is at the moment. All that I can express to you is my deep concern about the woman I am committed to spending the rest of my life with."

He turned to face one of the cameras straight on, "I am asking you. No, I am *begging* you, America. If you have seen Eleanor Quinn, please contact me. I am going to post a number on the screen. I know the world loves Eleanor almost as much as I do; we are all rooting for her safe return home."

Cheryl wiped a tear from her eye. Maybe she and Art used the same acting coach.

"We are in this with you. We will tweet out this contact information as well. Together, I believe that we can help save Eleanor. Let's get #bringEleanorhome trending."

With one last dramatic breath, Art mustered, "I can't tell you how grateful I am, really, thank you."

And with that, the screen cut to commercial. I stopped myself just short of hurling Kristy's Seahawks Super Bowl XLVIII mug across the room. Art Bishop had ruined my year, and now he was ruining my chance at starting over.

February 9th

Eleanor

The day before the album's release was tense, to say the least.

James felt as if he had somehow been demoted to a full-time babysitter. He spent half his time assuring the label that everything was okay and the other half of his time trying to make Art and Eleanor look like a real couple. In the last twenty-four hours, their mutual hatred seemed to have increased exponentially. There was so much drama: Chip was melodramatic, Art was demanding extra attention, Eleanor was argumentative, and Jenny was on the edge of a nervous breakdown. Then, in the evening, he had his *own* needy kids to deal with. It was exhausting.

That week, Chip had confronted Art and James, once again, about his lack of playing time on the album. He was the better pianist by a mile, but he was forever stuck on the guitar. Art insisted he should play any song featuring an instrument he knew how to play. Chip had had enough. He had talked it over with Jenny, who had nervously agreed that Chip was the better musician and should say something to James. So, he had.

And then, two days before their album dropped, Art had been featured in a magazine surrounded by instruments with the headline, "Art Bishop, what can't he do?" It was a punch in the gut to Chip. James insisted that it was fluke timing. Art didn't acknowledge the feature at all, which made things worse.

Chip was furious. Art had spent the whole interview talking about his debt of eternal gratitude to his music teacher. He'd praised the teacher who had inspired him at a young age to learn guitar and piano. He barely mentioned the band, and not once did he mention the fact that his beloved music teacher happened to be Chip's mother.

On her end, Jenny was indeed on the verge of a nervous breakdown. Since Art and Ellie had officially become a couple, all she could think about was the band's impending breakup. It seemed inevitable now. There was no way Art would set aside his ego once the relationship was over. There was no way that he was going to let this be an easy breakup. She had seen the way he treated women; it wasn't really a secret. She doubted that James had actually thought this relationship plan through. Ellie might love the band, but she also had a backbone, and Jenny knew that she would reach a point where she would have to draw the line. And that would be the end of it. The band would be done. They were quickly heading toward being the American version of ABBA.

Jenny honestly didn't blame Ellie for the band's impending breakup. If she were in her shoes, she would do whatever it took to be free of Art. Jenny avoided Art whenever possible unless Chip was with her. Sure, she had known him basically all her life, but that didn't mean that she was willing to look past the fact that he was a manipulative creep. Still, Jenny was not ready for the end of Kittanning.

Art was pouting. He had clearly drawn the short end of the stick. Actually, he had not "drawn" at all. He was being strong-armed into this situation. He had been making his displeasure clear to James all week. James kept promising he would make it better but never actually did anything. The night before had made him furious. Eleanor was a pathetic tease, and she was keeping him from living his best life. Life in a relationship was not one he wanted, especially not when he was in the middle of an album release. The girls always flocked to the Billboard-topping artists.

On top of that, Chip kept asking to play more and more in-strumental parts, which felt like he was not-so-subtly trying to take over the band. He had always known that Chip was jealous of him, which he couldn't blame. Chip had always been second to Art, and honestly, Chip wouldn't have been able to make it in the music industry by himself. It was a simple fact; he was just not as good as he thought he was. Sure, his mother was a music teacher, but that did not automatically make him the star pupil. In fact, Chip should have been way better than he was now. Art had had to work twice as hard without nearly as much help as Chip, and it showed. He was a much better musician now. Chip just thought that he was great because James didn't have the heart to tell him otherwise, and Jenny would stand by his side no matter how ter-rible he sounded.

Eleanor's hatred toward Art had indeed increased overnight. Every time she saw his arrogant face, she felt angry. How could he justify treating someone like he had treated her? Getting dressed that morning, she had seen the proof—marks she couldn't unsee reminded her last night hadn't been a bad dream. But each time she saw him or thought about him, she also felt a twinge of shame. How could she have let this happen? Sure, Art was a jerk. Everyone who knew him well knew that. But she was the one who had not been more direct. She was the one who had agreed to go to his apartment. Maybe this whole thing was more her fault than she had initially believed.

This week was supposed to be exciting. Usually, Eleanor loved the thought of releasing a new album, words that she wrote being put out into the world. Instead, she just felt ashamed of who she had let herself become. The woman who wrote those words would not have allowed herself to be treated like this. Her old self had a backbone. This new Eleanor would do almost anything that was asked of her. This Eleanor was just a shell.

James had booked them on *Saturday Night Live* the Saturday after the album dropped. The twenty-four hours leading up to *SNL* felt like chaos.

The album was released without a glitch. It was doing better in the charts than the label had predicted. James mostly credited this to the hype that was still surrounding Eleanor and Art's relationship. Eleanor credited it to good writing and the band's performance of the songs.

Who knew for sure what had caused the success?

James had made an executive decision regarding the songs they were going to play during the show. They would play two numbers, the first being "Home." This was the obvious choice for everyone. For the second song, he decided that they were going to play "Done My Time." Everyone was shocked.

"I didn't even think this song was going to be a single!" Art stormed into the studio, where they had all been preparing. It was Saturday morning, and he was clearly hungover from his night out with Eleanor. They had to get a drink together after the release party, according to James. They needed to be photographed together, celebrating. Since the incident earlier that week, Eleanor refused to even cross the threshold of his apartment. He could not believe that she was so dramatic. After she had left him for her own apartment, Art had felt angry. Four drinks later, he felt angrier, realizing that he would be spending the night of his album's release drunk and alone in his apartment. If it weren't for her, he could have spent last night with any woman in New York. And this was all her fault.

"'Done My Time' wasn't going to be a single, but it is now. It's one of the most-streamed songs on the album." James said sternly. This was clearly not up for debate.

"It is moody and sad." Art said, matching James's stern tone.

"It is a moving song."

"Thank you," Eleanor piped up from the corner of the room. She was not too thrilled about it being a single either, but it was one of her favorite songs she had written. She was just worried that its release would require her to talk about her sister, which was not a conversation she was going to have with the public.

"You can thank yourself, Art, for the hype," James added.

"Why's that?" Eleanor and Art asked at the same time.

"Apparently, at the party where you two announced that you were dating, you told someone that it was while working on that song that you fell in love with Eleanor. You had some cute story to go along with it. The reporter bought it. In her album review, she wrote that she was waiting on pins and needles to hear the song that had inspired her favorite relationship of the year."

"You have got to be kidding me; she bought that crap?" Art asked. He remembered his story now. He had been saying whatever he thought the lady would buy. He knew that she was a sucker for a good love story, which is why he had made it up in the first place. Really, this was the interviewer's fault for being such a schmooze.

James had worked with the set designers to have the lyrics scroll behind the band as they sang. He thought that it would help people to contemplate their deeper meaning. Simple, powerful, and to the point. Eleanor and Art would start at opposite ends of the stage and slowly work their way toward each other as the song progressed. It was cheesy and over the top, but people would remember it.

That evening, as she was getting her makeup fixed one more time, Eleanor still couldn't believe she was doing this. She was lying about the meaning of one of the most personal songs she had ever written. The whole thing made her sick to her stomach.

She didn't have much time to process what had happened before she suddenly found herself on stage, pouring her heart out to this crowd of eager strangers.

I've done my time
I've paid the highest price.
But I can't spend one more sleepless night without you,
I've done my time, I've done my time.

So please come, meet where I stand.
Oh, love, please come,
I need someone to hold my shaking hands,
Because I've been locked out, I'm on the ground; my tears no more
make a sound.
Trying to do this on my own
I'm alone in this prison cell of walls that I built myself.
Without you
I've done my time, I've done my time.

Oh, you know that I've tried.
To stand up on my own
But you know that I'm tired.
From doing this life alone
I've done my time
I've done my time
I've fallen hard
I pushed you away
But from down here on my knees, I'm begging you.
Please stay

So please come, meet where I stand.
Oh, love, please come,
I need someone to hold my shaking hands,
Because I've been locked out, I'm on the ground; my tears no more
make a sound.
Trying to do this on my own
I'm alone in this prison cell of walls that I build myself.
Without you
I've done my time, I've done my time.

Please don't leave
Please don't leave
Because I can't do this without you
Please don't leave
Please don't leave
Because without you, there's no me

So please come, meet where I stand.
Oh, love, please come,
I need someone to hold my shaking hands,
Because I've been locked out, I'm on the ground, my tears no more
make a sound.
Trying to do this on my own
I'm alone in this prison cell of walls that I build myself.
Without you
I've done my time, I've done my time.

The whole band sang the last line together without any instruments. It was beautiful and stoic. At that moment Eleanor knew: the people loved this artificial reality.

There was no way they were going to let her out.

September 2nd

Cynthia

Oh. My. Gosh." It was the only thing Kristy or I had been able to say for the past ten minutes.

We were both sitting there, staring at a now-blank TV.

"I have to get ready for class." It was the only thing I could think to do. I couldn't just sit there all day, reliving the words he had said about me.

"Wait. You're going to leave the house?"

"What else am I supposed to do?"

Kristy stared at me like I'd sprouted a second head: "He just put out a call to the whole world to find you."

I shrugged, "People look like celebrities all the time. Why in the world would I have run away from my very successful band—mentally unstable or not—and enrolled in a writing class at a small college in Washington? That makes no sense. It's the perfect cover! Plus, if anyone *did* suspect me, I think it would look more suspicious if I suddenly stopped going to class."

"I am only going to say this once because if I don't say anything and something bad happens, I will not be able to live with myself: I think you're pushing your luck on this one."

Deep down, I knew she was right, but I was not about to admit that out loud. That would be like acknowledging defeat.

"Thank you for sharing your opinion," was all I could manage before leaving to get ready.

As soon as I closed the bedroom door behind me, I felt my body collapse against the door, and I started to bawl.

From the other side of the wall, I could hear Kristy gathering her lunch supplies. If I could hear her, I was sure she could hear my sobs; but once those floodgates were open, I couldn't seem to stop.

A few minutes later, I heard a soft knock on the other side of the door.

I scooted forward so she could open it.

Without a word, Kristy sat down on the floor, put her arms around my shoulders, and let me cry it out.

I had to go to class. Feeling dehydrated and exhausted, I was very grateful to know that college did not require much, or any, effort to get ready. Pulling my hair into a bun, I splashed some water on my face and shuffled out the door. I felt like I was walking in a fog when I met Randy at his car.

"I have no words this morning," was all I could muster in greeting.

Randy smiled sympathetically, "Do you want to hear some?"

"Sure," I had to smile. Just from knowing him a few days, I knew that Randy was not really one for silence.

"Great." He proceeded to tell me the story of how he met his wife. By the time we arrived, I was laughing, almost forgetting about the daze that had enveloped my morning.

The campus felt less scary than it had yesterday. Even if this was only my second time walking this route, it already had hints of familiarity.

I walked into the classroom and sat one seat over from the aisle, leaving the left-handed desk open.

"You learned from yesterday," I heard Gabe's voice from behind me. I couldn't help but smile. Although I had zero recent experience making friends at school, I was hoping that he would consider himself my friend.

He told me about his morning. His bus had been late, which had caused him to wonder why he didn't just give up and start biking to class, but on his uphill walk to the classroom, he had been reminded that Seattle has hills.

It was so normal. Gabe's life was so normal that I felt a twinge of jealousy.

I was relieved when class started before he had time to ask me how my morning was.

"Where are you headed?" he asked as we started packing our backpacks.

"Home," I said simply.

"Do you not have a class after this?"

"This is the only class I'm taking. I enrolled late, and this was the only class left." It was not a total lie, although it was not the full truth, either.

"Wow, lucky you." We started walking out of the classroom together. "Do you like tacos?"

"What kind of question is that: 'Do I like tacos?'"

"I don't know, you're from Pittsburgh; I thought maybe there was a ban on good food there."

I rolled my eyes. "Yeah, yeah, I get it, you don't like Pittsburgh."

"Couldn't even pretend to. But I was going to say that there is a bar in Queen Ann that does a great taco night . . . if you like tacos." He winked. "A group of us are meeting there tonight if you want to join. I know you're new in town, so it might be nice to meet more people."

I could have cried. Given the emotional rollercoaster of my day, I could not believe that I might be able to get a glimpse of normalcy. But then I thought of Kristy and how worried she had been this morning. James had her number, after all. I didn't want to do something to put my new life at risk.

"Can I bring my cousin? She's actually my roommate."

"Sure, the more, the merrier. Hey, my class is that way, but if you give me your number, I'll text you the address."

"This is embarrassing, but I have to check my new number; I got a new phone when I moved," I explained, pulling my phone out of my bag.

A few awkward moments later, I gave him my number and started walking toward Randy's car.

When I checked my phone after getting in the car, I saw that he had already messaged me, *It's Gabe, your left-handed Seahawks friend. :) See you tonight!* followed by the address.

I couldn't stop a smile from spreading across my face.

"Well, do you have any words now?" Randy said with a smirk.

I couldn't tell him; I thought it might kill the magic.

I called Kristy when I got home to tell her the newly formed plan.

"Wait, I have so many questions. Firstly, oh my gosh, tell me all about Gabe!" She gushed. I forgot that I had not told her about him due to the Art interview drama. "Okay, I bet he likes you. I mean, who asks a girl to join him for tacos after meeting her only twice?"

I was grateful she chose to focus on the good instead of reminding me of the terrible morning I had suffered.

"Maybe I just make a good first impression? All that yellow must make me stand out. And plus, he was totally up for me inviting you."

"Yeah, right, he likes you," Kristy smirked.

"Okay, moving on . . ." I could feel myself blush. "Tacos. Are you free tonight?"

I could hear her checking her calendar.

"Yeah, I can be. I was supposed to meet up with some girls from work for drinks, but for the sake of your love life, I'll move it around."

"I love you."

"Yeah, I am adding this to the growing list of favors you owe me." She paused, her voice going serious. "You're sure that you're comfortable going out? The interview was today, you know?"

I sighed, "I knew you'd ask that. The thing is, the situation might get worse, I don't know. I want to be able to do these things now before this gets all over the news. There's a chance that people haven't heard yet. Like, do people even watch the morning news?"

"Okay, it's your call! I'll come home after work, change, and then we can go. Does that work for you? Wait. Do you have something to wear? You can't wear a sweatshirt out!"

"Oh, I didn't even think about that. There's always my sequined stage costume," I joked.

Kristy choked, "I don't think that would qualify as blending in. Think 'college girl.' You can go through my closet; I'll just add it to the list of favors you owe me."

"Love you, Kristy."

·❦·❦·

It was weird having nowhere to go. I could do whatever I wanted to do, yet I somehow couldn't find the motivation to do anything at all. Never in my life had I had so much downtime.

I realized having this class gave me some purpose. I didn't really know how to write anything but lyrics.

I thought about all the songs I had written recently. They all had a deeper meaning that I was never really able to share. Every song had felt like a piece of my soul was being divided and scattered. I had picked each word purposefully to get my point across without giving too much away. It had felt like a game to me, and I genuinely loved it.

My dad used to say that you don't really know something until you can say it in other words. Writing lyrics was always taking these stories and experiences that I knew and putting them into other words.

I looked over the prompt for our first assignment. This week, we were supposed to write a short story about our childhood. I thought about a song I had written about my grandma's house.

Art had hated it. He had only let it on our second album's extended edition because my grandma had just died, and he had known her.

That was the first time I realized my relationship with Art was deeply broken. Or maybe Art was deeply broken. He had spent so long fighting against releasing this song on the album. Then, just a few weeks later, he took credit during an interview for advocating for the song. He claimed I had been worried about releasing it because it was obviously about my family. We were going through something profoundly personal. He said he had told me including it on the record was the brave thing to do. He took credit for "convincing me" to share it with the world. He said that he had loved my grandmother, that she had been like a grandmother to him, and it would be a disservice to her memory to not release the song. All I could do was sit there and watch in horror mid-interview, doing all I could to keep a straight face. In interviews, we had learned to always have a "yes, and" attitude. It was bad etiquette to go against what someone else in the band was saying. I had no choice but to sit there and listen.

When the reporter asked me if this was true, I just said the truth: how deeply we had all loved my grandma and that we had all spent time around her dining room table as kids.

When I thought about this song and about what my grandma had meant to me, it was the best representation of my childhood I could think of. It was a nostalgic ballad meant for the guitar. I had written it so that the lyrics were sung as if they were being rushed, as if singing them faster would get you closer to a few more moments with the person who is lost.

I pulled up the lyrics from my phone and rewrote them on the page. I decided I would base my short story off this song.

It's not a house
More than a home
It's my childhood memories played out in front of me like a kid
come back home.
It's not a house
This is my home
We would spend our Friday nights around the table.
When we were willing and more than able
To deal with ourselves in one more time.
It didn't matter, no, it didn't matter.
If I lost every game we played.
It was about the memories we made.
In this house
Where you welcomed me home.

Too many times
This place was my saving grace.
From all the pain
The world, it can be so cruel.
You would always have
Cookies in the jar
Cards on the table
And the lotto playing on TV.
In this place
When it was you and me

We would spend our Friday nights around the table.
When we were willing and more than able
To deal ourselves in one more time.

It didn't matter, no, it didn't matter.
If I lost every game we played.
It was about the memories we made
In this house
Where you welcomed me home

You tell me how
I grew up so fast
Too many years pass
How old was I now?
My daddy must be so proud.

You built this house.
You made it our home.
And now God's arms
Are welcoming you to his own

But I miss those
Friday nights around the table
When we were willing and more than able
To deal ourselves in one last time.
It didn't matter, no, it didn't matter.
That I lost every game we played.
It was about the memories we made
In this house
Where you welcomed me home.

I wonder what my grandmother would have thought about this mess. I had only called my parents a few times since being at Kristy's. I called them from her phone every few days. Every call felt like a risk. I probably needed to call them tomorrow; they would no doubt have seen the interview. A wave of homesickness hit me.

I realized that James didn't know that I had a new number; it was not registered under my name. It was a burner phone, and we had put it on Kristy's card, just to be safe.

The sickening twist of homesickness dragged me down. I couldn't even call my parents today; I was sure they were freaking out and enraged right now. I wouldn't be surprised if they were on the phone with Art's parents demanding that he retract the interview. I didn't have the emotional space to have the "I tried to tell you he is the worst" conversation with them. I didn't want to be yelled at about how I had let Art ruin my life, but I needed to hear a familiar voice. I decided to call my brother, Adam, instead. I could count on him to always be in my corner.

"Hey stranger," I said when he picked up.

"Oh my gosh, El, how are you? How are you calling me? Mom said that you were with Kristy but that it was all top secret."

Just hearing his voice was enough to make me tear up.

"Hi, yes, I am okay. I am with Kristy, it's okay. But yes, very top secret. You can't tell anyone. Also, my code name is Cynthia. I'm starting over, and I figured when people run away in the movies, they always have a fake name."

"Can't argue with that logic."

"Did you see the interview?"

"Maggie and I watched it this morning. Sorry . . . what a jerk. I remember, even as a kid, Art was super arrogant. And like, what terrible things to say about you!"

"Yeah, it really sucks—he really sucks."

"So, what are you doing now that you are not, EQ, musical genius. Who is Cynthia? Other than a couch-crashing Seattleite."

"Cynthia has a bed, thank you very much. She is taking a writing class at a local college, like a normal twenty-something. And she is very grateful for her cousin who took her call at 8:00 a.m. to pick her sorry self up from a Greyhound station."

"Cynthia travels via Greyhound?"

"Yes, she is not good at planning her own travels. She grew up spoiled and having everyone plan everything for her; it's a rather annoying personality trait, but she is figuring out how to do things on her own."

"Welcome to the real world, Cynthia."

I changed my clothes at least five times before Kristy got home. I wasn't sure what I was supposed to wear. My whole identity felt fuzzy and unclear; I missed my own chic wardrobe. Last year, I had been voted one of *People's* most stylish celebrities. I thumbed through the rack, settling for the first thing that felt familiar. It wasn't that I didn't like Kristy's clothes; they just weren't mine.

I felt a nervous excitement as we drove to the bar; I couldn't stop fidgeting. I didn't want to admit to Kristy that I was apprehensive about this.

"Tell me about your day?" I asked. "Other than this morning, obviously. We can skip that bit." It felt like years ago that we had been sitting on her couch, watching Art single-handedly try his best to ruin my life.

"Well, I have recently switched teams. So now I'm working with Alexa. I can't tell you a lot about what we are doing, but I am so excited about this project. I really like my team. There is this guy on my team, Jake, who brings his dog to work. So that always makes the day better."

"Jake makes the day better, or his dog does?"

She rolled her eyes. "I mean, he doesn't make the day worse."

"You should have invited him to taco night!"

She just laughed.

"I'm serious," I argued. "Or we could have a picnic in the park or a wine night this weekend: I just love love!"

"I don't love him!" she shot back quickly.

I narrowed my eyes. "But you could."

"Yeah, maybe." I knew even without looking that she was blushing. "Anyways, so there's Jake and his dog, and then I ate lunch with some of the girls I used to work with, which was fun. Just a regular day."

"Do you like your job? Like, is this your dream job?"

"I don't know if this is my dream job forever, but for now, I like it. I don't think as a kid I dreamed about working for a company like Amazon. But I like working on projects that I know are helping people; this is one of those. I think no matter what I do, I just want to make the world a little bit better."

We didn't talk for a few blocks.

"What's your dream job?" she asked in return.

"I had it. Performing music was my dream job. Now, I'm not sure what I am supposed to do."

"Who knows? Maybe you'll write the next great American novel."

A few minutes later, we walked into what I imagined people talk about when they talk about going to a dive bar.

"This brings me back to college," Kristy said, motioning to the sticky floor.

It was disgusting, but no one seemed to mind. Everyone seemed relaxed, not to mention twenty-five or younger. I was starting to regret my outfit choice.

First, I was the only one in the bar who was wearing heels. I instantly felt like everyone was looking at my feet. Most of the girls in the room were wearing some version of skinny jeans and a slouchy top. In addition to my heels, I had on a yellow high-waisted skirt and a floral crop top. I felt like I had misread the invitation to a themed party.

Gabe saw me first and waved us over. He was dressed down in a graphic tee and worn jeans. My heart did a backflip: casual Gabe was undeniably cute. He hopped off his stool, grinning widely, and pulled me in for a warm hug. I was so taken aback that I froze, my mind racing. What did I do now? Other than Kristy holding me while I cried, I hadn't voluntarily hugged anyone since the last time I saw my parents. My mind flashed back to Art picking me up and spinning me around—my life imploding—and my spine instinctively stiffened. Gabe pulled away, quickly covering a flash of confusion with a welcoming smile for my cousin.

"Hey," I tried to say coolly. "This is my cousin, Kristy!" I added as we inched our way into the circle the group had made around the bar table. I found myself elbow-to-elbow with Gabe. From this vantage point, I could see the faded Star Wars logo on his shirt.

"Cynthia," Gabe motioned to the group around the table. "This is Jeff, Karen, Monica, Marshall, and Joe. We are all in the master's program together. Guys, this is Cynthia; she's in that writing class I'm taking. She just moved here from Pittsburgh, so go easy on her."

"I didn't realize that you were getting your master's degree; why are you in that English class?"

"Ah, well, my English credit from my last college didn't transfer, and I needed an English credit for my master's, so I picked the easiest one I could that worked with my schedule."

"What do you guys study?" Kristy asked. I was glad she was the one who had asked. I honestly hadn't even thought of it.

"Accounting," one of them—maybe Joe—responded.

The conversation started to flow. Obviously, they were all friends and had a good rapport established. Kristy and I interjected from time to time, which I was more comfortable with anyway.

Someone asked Kristy about her field, and they all seemed impressed by her job. I knew that she was smart, but it was nice to have context for what she did.

"So, why did you move from Pittsburgh?" Monica asked me.

I had been hoping to avoid this question all night.

"The weather," I quipped. Everyone laughed.

"Seriously, other than the better football team and sunny skies, what brought you out west?" Gabe asked intently.

I thought for a minute.

"I had been working the same job for a while, and I just had this wake-up call a few months ago. I really didn't like my boss, and I felt like I was losing a piece of who I was. So, I moved in with Kristy and decided that I might as well further my education while I am trying to figure out my next move." It was a truth-ful-enough answer.

"Man, a bad boss is the worst. I almost sold my soul to one. I've never been happier than the day I gave my two weeks," Joe—it was definitely Joe—added.

Everyone chimed in with their own terrible boss stories.

"So, what made him bad enough to move across the country?" someone looked at me and asked. I had been the only one to not share a lousy boss story.

I grimaced. "He kept taking credit for all of my work. I would pitch an idea, and he would take it as his own. I realized I was never going to be promoted because he was getting the credit that I had earned."

"Man, that's the worst," someone said, which got a lot of sounds of agreement.

The night went on, and I felt myself relaxing. I might actually be able to make friends. This was a significant development in my fight for normalcy.

At one point, Kristy and I went to the bathroom together, and the door had barely shut before she gushed, "He totally likes you!"

I blushed. "You think so? I think he might just be a genuinely nice guy. I don't want to assume."

"Fine, you don't have to assume, but I saw that hug . . . he likes you!"

The night was filled with so much hope; it felt like a full 180 from this morning.

Back at the table, I was lost in daydreams about a future in-volving my new friends and me when Kristy elbowed me.

"Ow, sorry, what?" I said when I realizing someone had been trying to talk to me.

"I said, how do you feel about karaoke?" Gabe asked slyly.

Oh my gosh. What if he knew? What if Gabe knew who I really was, and this was why he asked me here? I was about to be outed in front of all these people. I could feel my face going red as I searched for a way out.

"I've never done karaoke," I said. It was a lie. But I was hoping that maybe he would let me off the hook.

"Fine, then you don't have to go first." I must have looked confused because he explained, "It's tradition—when it's after nine, it's karaoke time!"

With that, Karen jumped up. "I want to go first!" She told the DJ her song choice and a few moments later, launched into a sour rendition of "Sweet Caroline."

"Promise you will at least *try* tonight; this is a great group for your first karaoke attempt, very forgiving," Gabe gestured to Karen on the stage. He obviously thought she was awful as well.

As soon as the song wrapped up, everyone started clapping. I wasn't sure if they were clapping for her or for the sheer joy that it was over.

A person from another table jumped up and started singing "Hey, Jude," which was one of my all-time favorite songs.

"I'm going next," Gabe declared. "How about this? We can do a duet; that way, you don't have to be up there alone for your first time."

I paused, shooting Kristy a panicked look. Kristy gave a mini shrug.

The table started chanting my name.

"Fine," I said meekly.

"Stage fright is normal," Karen assured me, eyes wide. "But trust me, there is *such* a rush when you're performing!"

Believe me, I wanted to respond, I know.

"Are you sure you want to do this?" Kristy whispered in my ear.

I nodded.

"So, what song are we going to sing?" I attempted to ask Gabe flirtatiously.

He answered my question by telling the DJ our pick, "Islands in the Stream."

"I love Dolly Parton," I said, blushing as he handed me my mic.

It felt strange in my hand.

The cheap lights felt bright on my face.

I wasn't wearing any stage makeup.

I hadn't warmed up my voice.

Then I realized that none of that mattered to anyone in the crowd. They weren't really here to hear me sing. They were here to have fun.

The sound of tinny piano chords filled the bar, and just like that, we were singing. It was hard to sing while ensuring that my voice didn't sound like Eleanor Quinn, but the different genre helped. Gabe was a much better singer than I thought he would be. Our voices entwined effortlessly on the chorus. It was fun and easy to be on the stage together, and we sounded kind of great.

The whole table was exploding with applause as we walked back to our table. Joe was whooping. Kristy looked relaxed for the first time since Gabe had announced karaoke.

"Wow, Cynthia, you sure can sing!" Karen said.

Gabe smiled over at me, "I was outshined for sure! You had me fooled by how nervous you seemed. You are a natural; you could moonlight as a karaoke bar singer!" Gabe added.

"Thanks," I said modestly. And with that, the conversation changed as the next person jumped up to volunteer.

February 17th

Eleanor

The world loved "Done My Time." After the band debuted it on *SNL*, it was rereleased as a single and quickly topped the Billboard chart. That was the first time one of Kittanning's singles had debuted at number one.

The whole thing felt surreal to everyone. For a few weeks after *SNL*, it felt like they were drifting on the coattails of that success.

And then it came time to finalize details for the tour.

This was the part that Eleanor really loved. This tour felt more urgent than the others. The end of the tour would mean the end of her and Art. Although they would be touring and spending all of their time together, Art and Eleanor could stop the forced public outings.

Since that night at Art's apartment, "dates" had been more tense and uncomfortable than ever. Eleanor was looking forward to never having to live through one again.

They announced their tour dates the week their album was released. Hours' worth of marketing meetings gave the tour a name:

Kittanning, Welcome Home. The irony made Eleanor a little sick. Jess had reminded her that there are many aspects to a concert that are like welcoming someone home. Someone going to a show felt invited into an inner circle, as they saw another part or side of the music. A concert should feel like home.

When she considered it from that angle, it warmed Eleanor's heart. That was what she wanted people to feel when they came to one of Kittanning's shows. She wanted everyone who walked into that arena to know they were seen and welcomed.

Their opener was a girl who had gotten famous on YouTube. Eleanor suddenly felt old. Their opener would be only seventeen when the tour started. It had never occurred to Eleanor that people could get famous on YouTube.

The first night of the tour would be two months from the album's release. Eleanor started counting down the days. She went to every tour-related meeting with an extra spring in her step.

Maybe, if she ever retired from music, she could help artists plan their tours. Not the logistical details but picking the set design, the costumes, and setlist. She loved this part.

Because the tour was titled Welcome Home, they were going to have a cozier-looking set. They decided that for the song "Home," they would bring two stools onto the stage, one for Eleanor and one for Art, and everything would be centered around this. It was supposed to feel like an intimate look into their living room.

In the middle of the living room style set decision, James segued to talking about the music video for "Home."

"Eleanor, you know that I have put this conversation off for as long as I possibly could, but we need to talk about the music video for 'Home,'" James said directly. Eleanor had the feeling this was not going to be a discussion.

She waited silently.

"We have hired a director, and we are going to start filming in two days. I put it on your calendar."

Eleanor was too mad to speak.

"What does Art think?" was all she could manage.

"He was the one who came to me with the idea. I'm sorry, Ellie, but you had been avoiding this conversation, and I needed to make a judgment call. I liked his idea and so did the producers. They fast-tracked the whole thing; we should be out by next Friday. All you have to do is show up and do what we tell you."

Both James and Ellie knew that was not all she would have to do. These things required more than anyone imagined, not including the emotional toll this would have on her. It was going to be two straight days of shooting.

Two days later, a car was sent to pick her up at 6:00 a.m. They were filming in an empty arena. It was in a part of town that she had never been to before. That was the thing about living in New York; it felt like she could spend her whole life exploring the city and never actually see it all. Maybe the city was telling her that she would never be at home here.

The idea of the video was to have everything stripped down. The band was shooting in an old, rusty arena. There would be a small stage that looked like it belonged to a county fair rather than a sold-out arena. Eleanor knew instantly there was no way the flimsy stage could hold all four of them plus instruments.

The video would be shots of each member of the band performing on the stage to an audience of one. They would sing to their significant other, who would be sitting in the front row of an empty arena. The lighting would be dim, almost yellow.

As much as she hated to admit it, Eleanor loved the concept. She also liked that it would honor Jenny and Chip, and not just be the Art and Ellie show.

She had two costumes for the show—one a stage outfit and one for when she was in the audience.

For her audience outfit, she got to wear an old Pitt sweatshirt, which she assumed was a tribute to their hometown roots, along with sweats and a pair of fuzzy slippers. She had never been more comfortable while shooting a music video, ever.

Her second outfit felt more like what she was used to. It was similar to the one she was going to wear on tour, a royal blue, covered in sequins—her favorite type of material. She loved seeing the glittering reflection out of the corner of her eye. It brought her joy. Even though it felt three sizes too small and was way less comfortable than her sweats, she loved it.

Maybe this wasn't going to be so bad after all.

James had also agreed to limit Eleanor's time spent shooting with Art, in part, because he had sprung the whole thing on her last minute. In total, they only had to be in the same room for five hours, which was not bad, all things considered.

A week after they had finished the shoot, James announced that the video was ready, thanks to some very hurried post-production work. They gathered in his office, where he had a big TV set up to play the video. Eleanor was determined to study the video to see if there was a noticeable difference between her and Art's interactions and Chip and Jenny's. She honestly didn't believe that she was a good enough actress to make her love for Art look authentic next to Chip and Jenny.

But somehow, it seemed okay. Ellie didn't look like a phony. In fact, it looked like she and Art were deeply in love.

In truth, the parts where it looked as if she was singing to Art, he wasn't even there. She had invited her best friend, Jess—the safest person—to fill that empty space.

The wonders of video editing never ceased to amaze her.

To Art, this video was the nail in the coffin to prove how deeply he and Ellie were in love. He could not have been happier with how the video turned out. This was all the proof he needed to show the world that they were on the same level as Chip and Jenny.

This idea had all been necessary for his plan. He needed to let Ellie see how much the world loved them together. If she saw what it looked like for them to be in love, she might actually start to believe she loved him. No one had to know that he had not even been sitting in the audience while she was singing.

Honestly, Art admitted to himself that his actions recently had been genuinely sacrificial. He had given up so much, surrendering his own talent and the spotlight so that she could also shine. He had also made sure to highlight Chip and Jenny, which he knew Eleanor would appreciate.

She should be more grateful to him. There was no way she would ever have made it on her own. His talent was much more obvious and natural. She needed him to support her. She would realize this soon, and he would never have to share the spotlight with her again.

The only one who would have made it on her own was Jenny. She was possibly the best drummer of the twenty-first century.

But she was cursed with being a drummer. No one, except other drummers, would ever buy an album of just drum solos. She had recognized this early on.

She was also the humblest member of the band. This might have been because she understood she needed them. She knew they were better together than they were apart.

Jenny was also the one who had united them. That detail often seemed to be lost when the band's story is retold.

It was true; they had all known each other since they were kids. That is what growing up in a small town does to you. There are no strangers, and everyone knows everything about everyone else.

Early on, Jenny knew that she was going to start a band. Not a small-town band. No, she was going to start a band that was going to go somewhere. As soon as she realized she was a better drummer than anyone she heard on the radio, she made this her goal and mission.

She had been dating Chip since before either of them actually knew what dating was, and he could play the guitar, so it was a given that he would be in it. Neither of them could really sing, so they would need someone else.

Jenny had let Chip in on her big plan. They would sit outside of his mom's music school and listen, trying to scope out the town's next big talent. This was where the trouble had started.

As soon as they heard Eleanor, they knew she was the real deal. Her voice, even unpolished, was effortless and easy on the ears. The power behind it was undeniable. It helped that she had been one of the nicest people in their class. If she didn't want to be a part of the band, she would at least let them down gently.

Much to Chip and Jenny's relief, she was happy and honored to be a part of their newly formed group.

There were not many places for them to practice their new music. If they wanted to play for a crowd who didn't know every member of their family, they had to go into Pittsburgh.

This detail was crucial. The band wanted to prove they were good, so they needed to hear from people who were not related to them. Pittsburgh was almost an hour away, so they could only play on Friday or Saturday nights.

After a month or two of making their weekend commute, word about the band got out. Somebody's mom must have blabbed to somebody else's mom. But somehow, one day, it was a secret, and the next, they were the talk of the town.

That was how Art found out.

Art was in their grade. However, he had been dating Eleanor's sister, who was a grade younger. This was another little-known detail. No one ever mentions that Art had dated Cora. To be fair, they didn't date long, and Art had been only a sophomore when they went out.

Art's dad was a sports agent. The Bishop family had picked Kittanning, Pennsylvania, to raise their children. Close enough for his dad to travel into Pittsburgh for work but country enough to raise a family. His father had connections to other agents, including people in the music industry.

And just like that, Art was in the band.

No one had known him well before he joined, but they knew him enough to know that his family had power, and they would need some sort of connection to make it.

This was another thing they never discussed—the real reason why Art was allowed in the band. They had needed him. Almost the month after he joined, they signed with James and their label. They were less than sixteen when this happened; it felt like a whirlwind dream come true.

Less than a year later, they had a song in the Top 40, "Never Mine to Love."

People said their big break was dumb luck, but Jenny knew the truth. Yes, she had worked harder than anyone would believe or imagine, but she also had the brains to realize she was a drummer. If she wanted to get the credit for her talent that she deserved, she needed a band. And as much as she hated to admit it now, she needed Art.

Art and Eleanor's sister broke up shortly after the band started working on their first album. They all switched to homeschool so they could focus on music. Eleanor and Cora's relationship was never the same after that.

Success is a weird thing. If you ask the average person, most will tell you that they want to be rich and famous and have people know their name. But then, if you are fortunate enough to make it big, whatever that might look like for you, there is a sense of nostalgia and longing for the way that life used to be.

And then, there are the people around you who knew you before fame came knocking on your door. There is almost a sense of entitlement that they, too, deserve to ride on the coattails of your success, for the simple fact that you had one math class with them in the eighth grade and once they lent you a pencil.

This happens to people who win the lottery. Once they are announced as the winner, everyone they have ever spoken to comes rushing to their door, reminding them of their amazing friendship. The promise of money has encouraged them to reunite with you, their long-lost best friend.

Fame is the same. You have your first Top-40 single, and suddenly, everyone and their mother wants a piece of the pie. And those who are close to you have even deeper expectations.

Cora was no exception to this rule.

Cora had grown up as musical as her sister. If anything, she practiced more, so she had a more professional sound at a younger age. She just wasn't in the right place at the right time. In fact, like half of their town, she also went to Chip's mom for music lessons: hers just happened to be after Eleanor's, so Chip and Jenny never heard her sing.

She was not as powerful a singer as Eleanor—no one was—but she had perfect pitch, and she was quite possibly prettier than her sister. Plus, she was more relaxed; Eleanor was so uptight about everything.

Somehow, Eleanor had been magically plucked away to be in the one band in western Pennsylvania that actually went somewhere. Somehow, in Art's mind, being in a band with her sister meant that he and Cora needed to break up.

This breakup should have been more devastating than it was for Cora. She wasn't mad at Art. If anything, she felt relieved to be free of the relationship. But she felt angry with her sister, who was now teaming up with the enemy.

Of course, Cora couldn't tell Eleanor about what she had suffered from Art. She felt so much shame, and they had both been so young. She thought maybe the way he acted was just immaturity. He would grow up into a better man. But, based on what she heard, Cora doubted that he had. Every time she saw him, she felt sick to her stomach—the way he would look at her, the way he would talk to her while no one was around, as if she had no actual value as a human being. She hated the person that he painted her to be. She felt cheap.

So, Cora stopped showing up. She didn't call her sister. Her beautiful sister had suddenly become a glamorized, alien version of herself. And, eventually, Eleanor stopped calling Cora as well. Cora wasn't sure if this made her feel better or worse. She felt a sort of power knowing that she had a "celebrity" begging to be her friend, even if that person was just her sister.

Overtime, Cora's hurt turned into bitterness. Her bitterness turned into resentment—her resentment into hatred.

Then, one day, she saw a picture of Kittanning. Her sister and Art were in the center of the shot, basically on top of each other. The headline had been something cutesy about how they were America's new sweethearts, the romance we had all been hoping and waiting for.

Cora felt sick.

Her sister had sold out.

Eleanor wasn't sure if the band's success made her sister resent her, but Cora had completely shut her out. She only called Eleanor when she needed something, which was rarely. The last time she had seen her was two Christmases ago. The evening had ended in a screaming match; Eleanor couldn't even remember why it had started.

Their lives had changed when Art joined the band, though he would never admit there ever was a band before him. They had only done a few months' worth of shows. They hadn't even really had a name. They just went by the "kids from Kittanning." That was how the bars had referred to them. That's how they got their name.

They wanted to always take a piece of their hometown with them wherever they went. At least, they were to lean heavily on that storyline while marketing the upcoming tour.

13

October 6th

Cynthia

I have friends. As pathetic a declaration as this might be, it feels like I have accomplished an impossible victory.

Almost a month had passed since Art's first interview. He was still campaigning, urging the world to help him find the escaped, mentally unstable Eleanor Quinn. However, I was almost able to drown out that noise because I had friends.

More than one: friends, plural, a whole group.

This was almost as euphoric as releasing new music.

Gabe and I were the closest by far. He was the only one I saw regularly because of our shared class. But Monica had made a habit of coming by Kristy's almost once a week, and the three of us started a wine night. We were currently tasting our way through the wine regions of France.

Gabe and I had developed a rhythm. I always got to class before him, on account of Randy's driving, but I would ensure his left-handed desk remained saved. Then, after class, we would stroll (and flirt) together until Gabe had to part ways with me to go to his next class. I noticed he lingered longer and longer each day.

Today, he broke our rhythm. I was more disappointed than I thought I would be. It was almost ten minutes into our class when he messaged me to say that his bus had never come, so he had to skip class today.

I text him: *Aw, sorry :(Don't worry, I'll share my notes with you.)*

This was somewhat of a joke because this class rarely required notetaking. If all courses were like this one, college would be a breeze.

My phone buzzed again: *Want to come over tonight and share them with me? I'll order pizza.*

My stomach flipped. I had never gone to Gabe's house before. Sure, I had hung out with him plenty of times but always in a public place. Going to someone's house felt more personal; you get an inside look at how someone lives.

Sure, does around 6 work? I felt a little bit of boldness.

Yeah, I'll text you my address.

I didn't take any notes. The only thing I could think about was that I had just said that I would go over to Gabe's house tonight. That adorable nerd had invited me to his house . . . tonight!

I felt like a middle schooler. I didn't care how pathetic my giddiness was.

Then, the reality of what a logistics nightmare I had agreed to hit me. I didn't have a car service anymore. I couldn't just call my driver and tell him when and where I needed to go. I only had Randy. I usually had Kristy; in fact, we always went out together. This would be the first time I would leave the house since Art's interview without Kristy or Randy.

I knew that Gabe lived off a bus line because he took the bus to class every day, but I didn't actually know how to take the bus. This seemed like something I should know how to do if I didn't have a driver's license. And getting a permit was not really an option at this point because that would be a dead giveaway to where I was.

I also didn't know if I should tell Randy. He probably had plans tonight. He has a life of his own, and this was such short notice.

As soon as we got into the car, I explained my situation as coolly as possible.

"Soooo, Gabe invited me over to his house tonight."

Randy nodded slowly. "Ah, your boyfriend?"

"My class friend, yes."

"That's cool." He clearly wasn't going to say anything else until I let him know where the conversation was heading.

I fidgeted with the straps of my bag: "But I don't know what to do. Like is it safe for me to go?"

"What do you mean is it safe?"

I hit him and immediately regretted it. It felt like hitting a brick wall. "I meant like will I be physically safe."

"Are you afraid of him?" Randy had a dangerous glint in his eye. "Because if he makes you afraid . . ."

"What? No, no, I am not afraid of *him*."

"Then what are you trying to get at?"

I paused. What was I trying to get at?

"Like taking the bus and then being in someone's house. It's just really risky."

"Why?"

"I can't tell you."

"That's right, I forgot you were European royalty," Randy said dryly.

I rolled my eyes.

I could trust Randy to be respectful and discreet. Kristy trusted him. He had safely driven me to and from class the last month.

He pulled onto my block. It was either now or never. Then I remembered that he had signed an NDA when he agreed to my madness.

"Okay, I am going to tell you, but you have to remember that you signed an NDA, and you cannot tell anyone."

He pulled up next to Kristy's building. "Okay . . ." His tone was weary.

I didn't know where to start.

"First, before I tell you, would you say that I am in a capable mental state? Throughout our month-long relationship, I haven't done anything that would lead you to believe that I should seek special help?"

Randy looked wary. "Nothing besides the cryptic nature of this conversation."

I laughed under my breath. I needed someone who didn't know who I was to confirm that I wasn't crazy, that Art was wrong. I needed to know what he thought before I could tell him the truth.

"Okay, so first, my name is not actually Cynthia. My legal name is Eleanor Quinn." I paused to see if he would recognize my name. His face didn't react at all. "Up until a month ago, I was a singer in the band Kittanning." Still no reaction.

I had at least thought that he would have some context; I didn't really think I would have to explain to him every detail of the last ten years.

"Have you heard the song, 'Never Mine to Love?'"

Randy shrugged. "I mean, maybe? I don't really listen to pop." That comment would have killed Art.

I started humming the tune, not even seeing a glimmer of recognition.

I sighed.

"You know, 'oh, oh, oh, oh, you're never mine to love, oh, oh, oh, oh, I thought I'd be enough, thought I'd be enough, but now I'm crying here on the floor wishing you would see me as more than someone who's your best friend,'" I sung a few lines from the chorus. "'That song. Have you heard it?"

He chuckled. "I've worked at a bar the last five years; of course, I've heard that song. I just wanted to hear you sing it. If I had a dollar for every time I heard some young drunk girl attempt to sing, 'Oh, oh, oh, oh,'" he attempted to sing the chorus, "I could retire."

"Great." I wasn't sure if I should take that as a compliment or not. "Well, I wrote that song. And that is me singing what is apparently an overly-catchy drunk girl soundtrack."

Randy's face shifted from confusion to recognition.

"Wait, *you* are the runaway pop star? Like the one who had every girl's dream proposal and then vanished? But Eleanor Quinn isn't a natural redhead. Even I know that!"

I nodded soberly. "Well, that's me. Me plus a bottle of hair dye, anyway."

"Oh my gosh, you *are* like royalty: the royalty of the music world." He fake-curtsied in his seat.

"Ha, ha." I rolled my eyes.

"So why are you in Seattle? Shouldn't you be off celebrating your shiny love and rising success?"

"Okay, remember that you signed the NDA, okay?" He nodded. I trusted him, I reminded myself, so I took a deep breath and opened up. "The whole thing was a sham."

"What do you mean?"

"Like we weren't actually dating; our manager set up our relationship because he thought it would help album sales."

"Wait, that actually happens?"

"Yeah, I mean in my experience, yes."

Randy winced empathetically. "Shoot, that sucks."

"Yeah, and the lead singer, Art, is a jerk on top of it all, which is actually why I ran. I mean, there was so much more going on than the world saw, but I had to get out, and so I did. Kristy is my real cousin, which is why I came to Seattle."

"Wow. Okay. So, what does this have to do with Gabe?"

"Well, Art basically told all of America that I was a danger to everyone around me and put out a worldwide search. I am worried about being caught. Like he basically made it seem like if anyone sees me, they have to turn me in." I started to cry. "Sorry," I sniffed. "He is just so manipulative. And I needed to get out of that relationship. I needed to start over where people didn't know who I was. I needed to be Cynthia and not Eleanor Quinn. I'm just worried that if I go to Gabe's, someone on the bus will recognize me, or somehow, it will get out that I am in Seattle. But I can't stop living life. That jerk took so much from me already; I won't let him control my every waking moment again."

Randy was silent for a full minute (I counted). I got to sixty and was about to awkwardly get out of the car when he said, "I can drive you tonight. I don't mind. It's a great excuse to go out on a date night. We'll pick you up at 5:30 to make sure you get there on time," he stated. "Send me his address, and we'll go out to eat nearby. That way, if anything happens, I'm there. No questions asked."

My tears returned.

"Thank you," I said meekly before awkwardly hugging him and getting out of the car.

I had seen Randy's wife once, just from across the restaurant at a bar over a month ago. I was looking forward to finally meeting her since I felt like I already knew her based on the stories that Randy told me each day.

Their car pulled up at 5:30 on the dot. I had been hoping they would be slightly late; I didn't want to show up at Gabe's right at 6:00. I thought that looked a little obsessive. After careful calculation, I figured that it would be best to arrive at 6:07. I knew I could not be early. He was always running late, and I didn't want to show up early and throw him off. I also didn't want to show up right on time, which would make it look like I was neurotic, but I didn't want to be too late, indicating that I didn't care.

It was challenging to find the right balance.

Randy showing up right on time was not helping my overall strategy.

"Hi, I'm Cynthia!" I said as I climbed into the back seat. I didn't know if I was supposed to shake her hand or hug her. Car greetings were one of life's unavoidable awkward situations.

"Hi," the woman in the front seat beamed. "I've heard a lot about you; I'm Sandrine."

She was just as wonderful as Randy had described her. Not that I had expected anything different, but sometimes people overplay the wonderfulness of their spouses. If anything, he had undersold her.

Thankfully, soon after we drove away from Kristy's, we hit traffic. This would put us back on track for a 6:07 arrival.

We chatted the whole ride about Sandrine's job and how she loved working with Kristy. She said that she was thankful that I had hired Randy because it had given them their evenings back. I hadn't even thought about how terrible his hours would have been at a bar.

I thought about all the security I had hired over the years and the crazy hours they were forced to work so they could match my terrible schedule. They had to travel with us, as well. I knew they had families; I talked with them about their wives and children, but I had never connected that they were giving up time with them so that I could be safe. Sure, they were being paid—but probably not enough.

If I ever toured again, I made a mental note to ensure the security team got a raise.

We pulled up to Gabe's house at 6:12. This was a better time outcome than I had feared when Randy picked me up. I knew showing up late was better than showing up early.

I don't know why I was so worried about this. We were friends. I was just hanging out with a friend . . . a charming, sweet, funny friend. I was wildly out of practice in the art of hanging out with friends, especially without the presence and security of Kristy.

It had started to rain, so I was glad when Gabe opened the door almost as soon as I knocked.

"Hey, sorry I'm late," I said hurriedly.

"No worries, rush hour traffic. Come in!" he said awkwardly, moving to the side of the door frame to let me in. "First, pizza. What type of pizza do you want?"

I had to think for a minute.

"Um, just a normal veggie one?"

"Wait, do you not eat meat?"

I could feel myself blush. "No, not really."

"Man, first you're a Steeler's fan, and now you don't eat meat." I could tell he was kidding, but it felt like every ounce of humor I had was dried up by my nervousness.

Thankfully, he quickly moved on to order our pizza.

"It'll be here in thirty minutes."

"Great, I'm starving."

Gabe sat on one side of the small couch while I looked around. I wasn't sure what I had thought his apartment would look like, but it wasn't really this. He had a matching couch and chair and a bookshelf that was overflowing. The whole room was spotless.

Above the couch hung a fiddle and a Martin D-28 guitar. Martin guitars were what I had played my whole life. On the last tour, I had played a Martin. I realized I didn't know what would happen to that guitar now that I was no longer touring. I felt a twinge of sadness. It was almost the same guitar that hung above that couch in my apartment in New York. That had been my favorite instrument I had ever played. It felt too special to allow it out of the safety of my place.

"Do you play guitar?" I said, motioning up to the wall above our heads. It would be a shame to own this guitar and not know how to play it.

"The guitar is actually my roommate's; I wish I knew how to play it. The fiddle is mine. I'm a closet fiddle player." He leaned in conspiratorially and whispered, "Don't tell anyone, but I love folk music."

My soul felt like it was flying; I had missed talking about music so much.

I sat next to him. "Can I hear you play?"

He looked at me reluctantly. "Really?"

"Yeah, man, I am expecting to hear 'The Devil Went Down to Georgia.'"

He reached up and took the fiddle off the wall, slowly, gingerly. It was the first time I had seen him act shy.

And then he performed "The Devil Went Down to Georgia" without missing a note. I had to remember to keep my jaw from falling to the floor.

"Okay, you can actually, like, *really* play the fiddle." I wasn't sure what I had been expecting; I didn't come across many people who were modest about their musical ability. Since he had been reluctant, I thought he would only be able to play a few chords.

Gabe's cheeks turned pink. "Yeah, I've been playing since I was like four. I don't know why. I guess I just love it. What about you, do you play any instruments? I mean, other than being a surprisingly great karaoke singer."

I couldn't help but smile at that memory. Since then, I had found myself craving a chance to perform again.

"I can play the guitar." I tried to hide that it took all my self-control to refrain from grabbing his roommate's guitar off the wall. "I can also play the piano a little. The guitar is my favorite. I've always identified the most as a singer, though."

Or I had been made to identify as a singer. I had to fight and almost audition any time I wanted to play guitar on stage or on the album.

I was saved from having to ask when Gabe reached up, grabbed the guitar, and handed it to me.

I could have cried. It had been over a month since I last held a guitar. It felt like catching up with an old friend.

"You know this is a really nice guitar, right?" I asked, raising an eyebrow. I wasn't sure if his roommate would want just anyone playing it.

"Oh, yeah, I'm sure he'd be fine with it. If you break a string, you just have to be the one to restring it."

"Deal."

I didn't know what to play; I felt so overwhelmed with joy.

I pushed my hair back from my face, "What do you want me to play?"

Gabe sat next to me, and our arms brushed. "Really, you think you are good enough to play whatever song I think of right off the bat?" He teased. "Hmmm, play 'Wonderwall!'"

"I don't see a campfire anywhere!" I laughed.

"You said any song."

"Fine," I complied and started singing along without thinking.

"Okay, I know that is the world's cheesiest song, but you are actually a really natural performer," he said as soon as I had finished the last chorus.

I almost responded, "Well, duh, that is my job," but I was able to catch myself before the words escaped.

"Thanks, I really love music," I replied instead.

"Okay, so seriously, what is your favorite song to play?"

I bit my lip. "You'll laugh at me."

Gabe laughed, "It's 'Wonderwall,' isn't it?"

"Oh gosh, no," I started picking out the chords to "Hey Jude." "I know it's supposed to be played on the piano," I said as soon as I

141

had finished, "but this is the song that made me love music. There is something about it—the lyrics and the melody that speak to my soul. I don't know," I shrugged. "This is good music."

Gabe was silent longer than usual. I had a moment of panic. Had I done the wrong thing? "I mean, I can play it on the piano. I'm sorry, I shouldn't have thought . . ." I started to backpedal and looked down at my feet, embarrassed.

"Hey, Cynthia." When I didn't budge, Gabe got off the couch and crouched in front of me. "Hey, where'd you go?" He waited for me to lift my head and make eye contact. "Are you seriously apologizing right now? That was . . . beautiful!" He paused again, "You should be playing at bars in town or something—you are outstanding." I could feel myself blushing both from the compliment and the sudden realization that Gabe smelled really good, like fresh air and pine.

"I'm not that good; it's just a hobby," I lied.

"My roommate has had that fancy guitar for years, and I have *never* heard it sound like that." Gabe was still looking at me intently, and my insides were slowly turning to goo.

"I am sure you are underselling his ability."

The doorbell rang, and Gabe jumped up to grab our pizza. Saved by pizza, I breathed a sigh of relief.

"Hey, can I ask you something?" Gabe said, a few slices into the pizza.

"No, I am not going to play 'Wonderwall' again," I said, teasing.

"Haha, no, something more serious than 'Wonderwall.'"

"More serious than 'Wonderwall?' I didn't know that existed! Yes, go for it."

Gabe set down his slice of veggie pizza. "This might sound like I'm reading into this way too much, but a while back at the bar, did I cross a line when I hugged you? If so, I'm sorry. I should have asked; it was a reflex."

I could feel my face flush with shame. Giving your friend a hug at a bar is a normal human interaction. It used to be normal. And then Art happened. Somehow, he had managed to tarnish even the most common human interactions.

"Oh my gosh, Cynthia, I am sorry. I didn't mean anything; I am so sorry."

I realized that I had teared up. This was so embarrassing. I felt a wave of fury rush through my body.

I took a deep breath.

"No, it is not something you did, Gabe." I paused, trying to pick my next words carefully. "The guy that I dated before I moved to Seattle, one of the reasons I left, actually . . . well, he was not a nice guy." I had to laugh to myself; that was putting it lightly.

"Do you want to talk about it?"

I grimaced, "Honestly, I'm not sure *how* to talk about it. I have had to be silent about it for so long." I took a deep breath. "You know what? Dating him was like suffocating, except no one knew my throat was closing but me. I couldn't say anything to anyone. I was afraid to speak up. It was all my fault anyway. Or at least, he told me that it was my fault.

I looked down at my pizza and added, quietly, "He told me I was nothing without him. Anyway, it was the type of relation-ship that ruined hugs, apparently." I tried to shake it off with a laugh, but Gabe was quiet. I wasn't sure if he expected me to say something else—change the subject or make a joke to lighten the mood.

Instead, he looked me straight in the eyes, "Cynthia. He sounds like he was abusive. That is not an okay way to treat someone, to treat you. I am so sorry that you experienced that."

He was abusive.

That was the first time I had heard those words out loud.

My fake relationship was abusive. Could that even qualify as abuse?

Seated next to me on this tiny couch was the antithesis of Art. Gabe, whose words and actions are everything Art's weren't.

We finished our pizza, and he walked me to the door, hesitatingly. This time, I purposefully leaned in first to hug him goodbye. I refused to let the feelings of shame control my life. I found myself not wanting to let go. This was what healing felt like: the pain, hard and cold in my chest, beginning to thaw. I could hear Randy's car pulling up in the distance. Gabe dropped his arms, looked at me for a moment longer than normal, and smiled. I couldn't help but feel a spark of hope as I ran through the Seattle rain to the car.

March 6th

Eleanor

Eleanor woke up in her own bed for the last time before leaving on tour. Her actual bed in her own apartment. Not the secondary option she had across town.

Leaving for this tour felt different than the tours before. It wasn't that she dreaded it, per se, but she didn't feel the typical pre-tour giddiness she should generally have on this type of morning. They would first be heading to Boston, where they were opening their tour.

They would do their East Coast leg first, followed by the South and West Coasts before doing a European leg.

She liked playing in Boston. She had played there before, and it was close enough that it almost felt like they had a home-field advantage. Plus, Boston was a big college town. They would get a super rowdy crowd, which was always good momentum for the start of a tour.

Eleanor was most excited for Pittsburgh, as was the rest of the band. That was going to be their third stop, after Philadelphia. Then, they would be back in New York for two nights. On the East Coast, New York and Pittsburgh were always her favorite shows. She could count on her people being in the crowd, cheering her on.

They were scheduled to leave for Boston this afternoon, then they would spend all tomorrow doing soundchecks before their first show the next night. They had been practicing and prepping for this moment for months. The start of a tour usually felt like a new beginning.

Her grandmother used to say that she could sense when there was something bad coming. Ellie, for the first time in her life, believed in her grandmother's ability. It felt like something was going to go terribly wrong. She had woken up that morning and had just known something was off.

Some clueless, underpaid staffer had assumed the band only needed two buses for the band members. There was one for Ellie and Art and one for Chip and Jenny. They had also booked a shared hotel room for Eleanor and Art on nights they were staying in a hotel. To be fair, this was not the staffer's fault. The fact that Ellie and Art's relationship was a scam was a secret. That secret was not to be mentioned within the walls of their record company. The people who knew the details of their fraudulent relationship were limited to a need-to-know list.

This was especially true now that the band was going on tour, leaving behind their carefully calculated ruse. When James saw the tour bus mix up, he made no effort to correct it. The fact that the "couple" was sharing a tour bus meant no one would question the relationship's veracity. It would also reduce the chances of Art getting cocky and inviting some random groupie into his bus or back to his hotel room. Not that James wasn't skilled with handling that particular issue.

On the last tour, James had been forced to hire someone whose job was to monitor Art's post-show behavior. He had always credited Art's behavior to the fact that Art was a "star." It didn't matter that he never had to worry about this type of attitude or behavior from Chip or Jenny or Eleanor. Three-fourths of the band did not act that way. Yet, he justified the behavior for the one.

On this tour, he didn't have to worry about that. He had someone on standby Art duty, just in case, but this tour had Ellie coupled with Art's new public image to ensure that he stayed in line. The tour might not have started yet, but James woke up that morning feeling at peace.

Chip and Jenny's feelings mirrored Eleanor's. They were both nervous about this tour. Jenny had already told Eleanor that she was welcome to sleep in their bus at any point. She had mostly offered because she understood the misery of sharing such a small space with a boy, even if he was her husband. Eleanor hadn't told Jenny how Art had been treating her, but Jenny could sense that something was wrong. Jenny had asked Chip about it. He had brushed it off, saying that no one in a relationship with Art would be totally comfortable. It was Art, after all.

Jenny didn't understand why everyone was willing to justify his actions just because of who he was. She didn't think she could say anything to Eleanor, in case she was reading into it too much, but Jenny wanted to make sure that she at least offered some relief.

Art had mixed feelings about the tour. He had a plan; he had thought it over, again and again, he had mapped out every detail, most of which had had to be planned months in advance. He had a notebook where he had kept all the details in order. He had lists of who knew what and who couldn't know anything. He hadn't told Chip and Jenny his full plan yet; he wanted to wait until all the pieces had fallen into place. If he had already booked something, they wouldn't be able to tell him, at least out loud, their thoughts about it.

Two nights ago, he had found the final piece of the puzzle. The Lumineers had confirmed, and they would be available to perform at the Denver show. He had immediately agreed; it was perfect. Denver's was a random enough show that no family would be there, so he didn't have to worry about their interference. The tour would have been going on for so long at that point that he could pitch it to James as a mid-tour press headline maker. He was always willing to do what was necessary to get good press.

It also helped immensely that The Lumineers were Eleanor's favorite band. He knew that would get him brownie points.

Chip would be an easy sell; he probably wouldn't even think twice about it. Jenny would be the difficult one. But he knew her Achilles heel: more than anything, she loved love. He would just need to prove, at least to Jenny, that he and Ellie were actually in love.

Art calculated that, for this to work, he would need to let her know the fuller extent of his plan in three weeks. This would give her enough time to see that Art and Ellie were genuinely falling in love with each other. This would also allow her enough time to get excited about the proposal—but not so much that she would accidentally let something slip to Eleanor.

If Eleanor even caught a whiff that this was happening, the whole thing would be doomed, and everything he had worked for would be for nothing.

He was officially on the clock.

15

October 17th

Cynthia

It had been eleven days since the guitar-playing pizza night, and the thought of how wonderful it had been still consumed most of my thoughts. Kristy was no help in this. Since the karaoke night, she had started obsessing about the potential new relationship as well. Despite her positive attitude, there was still a piece of me that believed we were imagining the whole thing. Gabe didn't really know me. Sure, we saw each other a few times a week, but that was just in the context of class.

There was also the very real fact that a relationship right now would be logistically impossible.

I was pretending to send an important text when Gabe walked into our class looking two hundred times happier than usual.

"Wow, you have a spring in your step today!" I said dryly.

He barely let me get the words out before he burst out, "What are you doing this Saturday night?"

"Like the Saturday that is four days from now?"

"That's the one—are you busy?"

I pretended to have to think about this. I didn't want to let on that my social calendar was wide open.

"I don't think I have plans. Why? What's up?"

"Great, this bar down the street from me is having an open mic night, and I think you need to play. And by that, I mean that I've already signed you up!"

Instantly my mind started spinning. I wanted to melt into my desk chair.

"Wait, you did what?" Maybe I had heard him wrong.

"Here's the deal: if you agree to this, I'll play the fiddle that night; we can conquer our performance anxiety together."

My mind was running. How could I salvage this conversation?

"Wait. New idea, what if we play together, like a band? That way, we'll be like a team!" I smiled hopefully. This felt like the best possible solution.

He thought about it for a few seconds.

"Okay, deal."

"Okay, so we need to come up with a setlist, and then we need to practice." My mind started switching back into Eleanor mode, running through all the steps required to form a band.

"Slow down, sparky. Do you want to come over tonight to practice?"

I remembered Randy had an event with Sandrine tonight. Kristy was also going to be there; it was a big celebration for their whole Amazon team. This meant that neither of them could drive me. I was not ready to attempt the bus alone, and there was no way I would risk taking an Uber.

"Would you mind coming to my house instead?"

"Yeah, sure, that's fine! Does seven work?"

"Perfect!"

⁕

"Randy, I need to make a stop on the way home, if that's okay?" I asked as soon as the car door closed.

"Of course, Your Majesty, where are we heading?" He laughed at himself. Every time he referenced my "royal status," he thought he was hilarious. I always rolled my eyes in response.

"Any music store. I need to buy a guitar."

He looked at me with equal parts shock and joy.

"I'm on it!"

Twenty minutes later, we had pulled into the parking lot.

"Okay," I whispered to him as we entered the store, "you cannot make any reference to me knowing anything about music. The guitar is for you, not for me. Got it? I'm just along for the ride. You are upgrading to a Martin D-28. Just 'yes and' him the whole time, act like you know what you are talking about."

"'Yes and' him . . . what is that supposed to mean?"

"Like the improv thing, everything he says, just agree and add to. It's improv."

"First, you want me to pretend to know something about musical instruments, and now suddenly, I need to know improv? I'm beginning to think you drastically mislead me with your job description. I am a bodyguard, remember?"

"Yeah, yeah, yeah," I said, ignoring him.

Everything around me was beautiful. I wanted to reach out and play each of the instruments that hung on the wall. This place felt the most like home since I had arrived in Seattle.

I pushed Randy toward a young salesman who looked less than eager to help us. He appeared to be calculating how long until his shift was over.

"Hi, sorry to bother you," Randy said, approaching him kindly. "I am looking to buy a guitar?"

"Well, a guitar store *is* the right place to buy a guitar," he quipped. "Do you know what you are thinking, acoustic, electric, bass?"

Randy shot me a panicked look. I had not prepared him enough for this outing.

"Didn't you write down the one you wanted?" I prompted.

"Oh yes, I am looking for a . . ." Randy glanced at the paper, ". . . Martin D-28."

"Really?" The salesman raised an eyebrow. "That's not really the type of guitar we would recommend to beginners. Why don't you try it out first to make sure it's a good match?" He pulled the guitar off the wall.

Randy held it awkwardly in his hands. I would not have been surprised if it was the first time he had ever held a guitar.

"Yes, well, it's actually for my daughter. Her birthday is next week, and she is an amazing guitarist. I called my cousin, and she said this was the best guitar for her." That was one way to "yes and" a conversation.

"Okay, in that case, I will make sure to print you a gift receipt." He headed to the register. That was when I realized I had forgotten to pull money out of the ATM.

"Randy, we can't buy the guitar here," I whispered to him. "We need to leave."

Randy didn't take more than a second to react. "Actually, my wife just texted me." He pulled out his phone. "She already came by and purchased it—miscommunication. I'm sorry, man."

The salesman didn't look surprised.

We left in a rush.

"What was that about?" he asked when we got back to the car.

"I forgot to get cash out. And putting a $3,000 guitar on my credit card might raise some suspicions."

"That guitar was $3,000?" He was shocked.

"Yeah, it's a really great guitar."

"Wow, who knew?"

I winced. "I'm sorry I wasted your time."

Randy just laughed. "Don't sweat it; today was confirmation that I am not about to pursue a career in music."

I had to text Gabe on the way home to ask if he could bring his roommate's guitar over tonight. If he wasn't able, I had assured him that we could still come up with a list of songs and practice with the fiddle. He responded, telling me to chill since this was just an open mic night.

Then, I called the only person I could trust in New York.

"Um, hello?" A confused voice picked up. I had known she would answer. If someone called Jess on her private line—even from a blocked number—she knew they were worth talking to.

"Hi, it's me," I said softly.

The other end of the phone was silent for a while, and then I realized she was crying.

"Your parents called me a few weeks ago and gave me the full update. You're in Seattle? Is it safe for you to call me? I don't even know where to begin other than to tell you I had no idea, and Art is a terrible person. I mean, I had no idea that he would propose, or I would have stopped it or told you. We all knew that Art was an idiot."

I realized I had started crying. I reached for a tissue.

"Yes, this is a prepaid phone line; I have only called like five people on it." I stopped to suppress a sob. "I know you didn't know; he didn't even tell my family about it."

"Of course, he didn't. I am so mad; this whole thing makes me furious. So, what are you doing? I obviously know you're not locked up somewhere going crazy, or whatever Art's lie *du jour* is. Did you hear that he tried to file a missing person's report?"

"Wait, really? Like an Amber alert for an adult?"

"Yeah, it was basically to strong-arm your parents into admitting they knew where you are. I was asked to sign it in solidarity. I didn't, of course."

"What did my parents do?" I was sure that Kristy knew about this but hadn't told me. I felt my stomach turn as I thought about how many people I had dragged into this with me.

"A representative for your family came back stating your family has had regular contact with you. They made it clear you left voluntarily and that you, therefore, didn't qualify as a missing person."

"Oh, thank goodness!"

"Seriously. Okay, so obviously, you're not missing, but what are you doing?"

"Well, I'm in Seattle. I moved in with my cousin Kristy; I think you met her at some point. Anyway, after Art proposed, I didn't know what else to do. Everything felt so overwhelming and confusing. Like, what is the protocol for when you are trying to get out of a forced fake relationship? I just hopped on a bus and headed north. I didn't have a plan—not that that should come as a surprise. I don't really know what I was thinking. But, yeah, I've been in Seattle, and I started taking an English class from a college here, just to have something to do each day. I am currently trying to figure out what my next move is."

"Okay, well, I am here for you. Whatever you need, just say the word. I have some time off right now, so I'm super flexible."

"Okay, so I have a confession and a favor to ask."

"Anything!" Jess was intense, but I could always count on her to be in my corner.

"I met this guy; it's not what you think . . . it's not romantic," I said before she started peppering me with questions, "but he is in my class, and he plays the fiddle. I don't know, but now it's this whole thing. So, he somehow convinced me to do karaoke with him one night and said something along the lines of how I was a natural on the stage."

"Duh, it was your job!" she said, cutting me off.

"Well, that is the thing, he doesn't know who I am. I cut and dyed my hair. So now I'm basically Amy Adams without the curves. I've only told Kristy and my bodyguard/driver the truth. This guy thinks I am just some girl who moved to Seattle for a fresh start."

"So, he thinks you are just some random twenty-something who decided to come to Seattle for a change of scenery, and it turns out that you are one of the best performers, slash singers, the world has known?"

"Okay, well, that is a bit of an exaggeration."

"But my point stands. So, what's the next move with the guy now that you have wowed him with your seemingly natural karaoke ability?"

"Well, that's the problem. Long story short, he signed us up to play at an open mic night this weekend."

"Wait, what! You're going to perform? On a stage?"

"Is that stupid? I know that Art has a manhunt out for me right now, and I don't want to be reckless, but also, this is who I am, you know? I got to play his roommate's guitar recently, and it just felt like I had found a missing piece of myself."

"I get it; I don't know who I would be if I had to walk away from the music." She paused, I could tell she was thinking about what to say next. "I think you should do it. What's the worst that could happen? If for some reason you are caught, at least you will be caught doing something you love."

I could feel myself breathe a sigh of relief. I wasn't crazy for wanting, needing to do this.

"So how can I help you with your comeback?" she asked. I could tell she was jumping around with excitement.

"Do you still have my spare key?"

"Yes, I do!"

"Great, I need you to go into my apartment and get my guitar, the Martin, and I need you to get it to Seattle by Saturday morning."

"I love this plan. I'm going to head to your house now. You, ma'am, can expect your guitar tomorrow! Send me your address!"

"You're the best."

"Hey, you know I am here for you; whatever you need, just say the word."

"I've missed you." It was all I could manage without crying.

•·ᴖ·ᵒᵉᴖ·•

"Okay, so, like I said, I don't have a guitar here," I admitted to Gabe later that night. "But I promise that I will have one by Saturday!"

"No stress. I mean, worst comes to worst, you can always play my roommate's; he doesn't need it Saturday."

"Yeah, but it's just not the same. Like, I am going to be extra nervous, performing in front of a crowd, and I just want to do it with my own guitar." I didn't tell him that my guitar, which would hopefully arrive by Saturday morning, had been custom-made and that I only used it on special occasions. I never brought it on tour with me just in case something happened to it. And I rarely got to play guitar live anyway.

"Okay, if you insist. So, we will have max five songs to play. Do you think that you have it in you? I mean, I know that is a long time to be on stage, but I think you are so talented that it will fly by!" He smiled warmly, and my heart stopped.

I was not used to being so encouraged regarding my talent on stage. It was weird but oddly refreshing.

"Yeah, that is what, like twenty minutes? I can do anything for twenty minutes! What about you? Are you feeling nervous?"

"This might sound so dumb, but I used to play in my school's band, so I am just hoping that my performance instincts will still be intact, like riding a bike or something. And like you said, it's only twenty minutes. And, bonus, I'm just the fiddler, you're the star of the show."

He played nervously with the fiddle in his hand.

"So," he said decisively, "I think we should open with 'Hey Jude' as a tribute to the song that made you love music."

I couldn't help but smile.

The next morning, Kristy was filling me in on her office party the night before over our morning coffee when there was a banging on the door.

"Who in the world is knocking at 7:30 in the morning?" she asked groggily.

"Oh! Maybe it is UPS; Jess is sending my guitar today."

"At 7:30?" She looked at me like I had never had a package delivered before.

"You never know!"

She opened the door. She was always on door duty. I lived in constant fear that I would open it and be greeted with a fan who had somehow figured out my location.

All I could hear was laughter as Kristy walked back into the kitchen with my guitar and Jess in tow.

Jess grabbed me up in a giant hug. "I can't believe you thought you could run away without a guitar!" She might have said more after that, but I couldn't hear anything over my tears of joy.

16

March 12th

Eleanor

Jess, I am telling you. Something is going on with Art." Eleanor paced around the parking lot. They were in Pittsburgh, getting ready to play for their hometown crowd. They had been on the road for five days. After one too many snide comments from Art, Eleanor had escaped to the parking lot to call Jess.

"What do you mean, like is he being more Art than usual?"

"No—yes, I don't know how to explain it. On local TV this morning, he said he can't wait to bring our baby to Pittsburgh. *Our* baby!"

Eleanor could hear the fury in Jess' voice. "Wait, he said *what*?"

"I know! We were in the middle of this interview. He just casually mentions that we're planning on bringing our children to Pittsburgh to experience the place where we grew up. And then, the whole car ride home, he kept talking about our future life. At this point, it was only Chip, Jenny, James, and me in the car—everyone who knows that this is a scam. He wouldn't let the subject drop."

"What would lead him to say something like that? You don't think that he is actually starting to like you, do you?"

Eleanor considered it a moment then shook her head.

"No, there is *no* way. I saw him making eyes at the interviewer just this morning. He has to have some ulterior motive."

"What are you going to do about it?" Jess asked sharply.

"I don't know. I can't let him win."

"What is he winning, exactly?"

"I don't know . . . whatever game he's playing."

"Well, keep me updated. I've got to run; I need to head to the studio! But if you need me to make the problem 'disappear,' you know how to reach me." It wasn't the first time Jess had offered to "take care of Art." Although Jess would probably do fine in prison—she'd be running the whole thing in a matter of weeks—Eleanor didn't believe in murder.

Eleanor made her way back into the stadium. She had a few hours before she needed to be at soundcheck. The arena was buzzing with people running around, setting up for the night.

Her family was going to be at this show. Her parents had also gone to the show in Boston; they always went to see the opening night no matter where it was. But tonight, her brother and sister-in-law would also come. She had invited Cora but hadn't heard back. She still left a ticket for her, just in case.

Performing in Pittsburgh was always her favorite, but it also meant that people would crawl out of the high school woodwork to get free tickets. If she had a dollar for every time someone asked her for, or just assumed that they were entitled to, a free ticket, she would be able to finance the full tour.

She focused on avoiding Art. She assumed he was on their tour bus. She still could not believe James had not corrected the tour bus mistake. The last thing she had ever wanted to do was share a bus with Art. He was always in their bus. She couldn't remember if this was how he acted before when he had a bus to himself. Was this habitual? Or was he only doing this to try to catch more time with Eleanor?

Either way, it didn't feel fair that she couldn't take a nap in her own bus in peace.

She thought back to their interview earlier that morning. The interviewer was probably their age. Eleanor had wondered if they had been in high school at the same time. The woman had gushed about her high school years in Butler, not far from Kittanning. Apparently, she remembered hearing whisperings about a band from Kittanning that was actually going to make it big. She joked that no one had believed it until the band's first tour.

"Well, you know us," Art leaned forward; Eleanor could tell he was about to start flirting with the interviewer when he quickly remembered where he was. He instantly pulled back. "We are just a little band from Kittanning."

"What does it feel like to play a show in Pittsburgh?" She gestured to the air around her, which Eleanor had assumed was supposed to represent Pittsburgh.

"For me, it's like coming home, really," Chip said, his eyes a little teary. He was a homebody through and through. "There is something about seeing Terrible Towels flying, being catered pierogis—man, this is the world's best city. I don't have any other words for it."

Jenny leaned forward, partially to comfort her now teary-eyed husband and partly to answer the question. "For me, this is when I realized that I am living my dream. I had always talked about starting a band. Being back here is a perfect reminder that my dreams have come true. It's perfect."

"As a kid, I would come into Pittsburgh every weekend with my dad," Art said. "Everywhere I go is a reminder of my favorite childhood memories. It makes me excited for my, or our—" he said, looking at Eleanor with an expectant smirk, "children to get to come back to this great city and see why we love it so much."

Eleanor was so shocked that Art had announced to the greater Pittsburgh area that he wanted them to have children that she forgot to answer. Art kicked her, rather hard, under the table.

She turned her grimace into a tight smile, "I don't know what to say that's not already been said. There is nowhere I would rather play than Pittsburgh. This is and will forever be my home."

•◦～ৡৢ৾ৢৎ～◦•

"What was that?" Eleanor demanded. They were back in their bus, out of the earshot of the others, whom he was clearly trying to convince of his deep desire to have a baby with Eleanor.

"What was what?" Art looked at her innocently.

"You want us to 'come here with our children?' What kind of line is that? And why did you need to spend the whole car ride going off about all the future plans you have for our unborn, un- conceived, children?"

"What is wrong with me wanting my children to see the city I grew up in?"

"There is nothing wrong with that. There is something wrong, however, with assuming that those children will also be my children."

Art backed up a step, "Are you saying you don't want my chil- dren?"

"How am I supposed to answer that question? No, Art, I don't want our fake relationship to include children. I just think that would make things a little too complicated," she said dryly.

"Just think about it," Art cajoled. "It would be such a good PR move. Our baby would be the talk of the town."

"Yeah, for like five minutes, and then the world would move on. And plus, I don't want to have a baby, let alone your baby. Do you know what that would do to my career right now?"

"I think it would be a better PR move than you are letting on; I think that you are just afraid to sacrifice your happiness for the sake of the band."

Eleanor shook her head in disbelief. "What do you think I've been doing these past few months? Do you somehow think this 'relationship' is making me happy? Are you happy?"

"You are so selfish, Ellie. Do you not understand how good this would make me look? Art Bishop: the doting father."

"Do you not understand how this would make me look? Eleanor Quinn: the mom who ignores her baby to go on tour!"

"Well, you would just take a break from touring." He said it as if it was the most obvious thing in the world.

Eleanor was too confused and angry to respond. Instead, she just stormed out.

·⁓·ᴗ˸⌒·⁓·

Admittedly, this was not how Art had meant to breach the subject. He had prepared a much sleeker speech to attempt to prove to her how good of a move having a baby would be for both of them, but Eleanor had ruined it. He should have come to expect this from her. She couldn't let things go. Not to mention, she refused to see things from another point of view. It was like talking to a wall. She refused to believe that having a baby would help Art's career and hers by association. Her stubbornness made him so mad.

She was *not* going to let this ruin her favorite night. It was just a fight. At this point in her career, she should be used to fighting with Art. But this time, it felt more personal. He was making plans about her life without thinking about how those plans might affect her. And she was a very crucial part of his plans.

She suddenly worried about what else he might blurt out during future interviews. And she wouldn't be allowed to react because, in theory, she would have already talked with Art about it. Because that is what you do in a relationship.

There was no way that she could spin this baby story her way. If she leaked to some tabloid that she didn't want to have kids now, she would be painted in a negative light. A woman was supposed to want to have kids, right? What type of woman would she be if she denied Art his desire to have kids? That was not going to look good. Then there was the fact that Art had, very strategically—she had to admit—made this comment in an interview. There was no way to claim that this was a misquote. The world heard him say it. There would no doubt be video evidence. He was the one who wanted to have kids. He was advocating for his future family.

She was the dream crusher.

After calling Jess and circling around the area, she still had time to kill. She decided to see if she could hang out in Jenny and Chip's bus.

·ᴄ～ᴗ°᛫ᴄ-ɢ～ᴐ·᛫

Jenny was the only one there when Eleanor knocked on the door.

"Good timing, I just woke up from a nap; I hate early morning interviews." Jenny was, and would forever be, a night owl.

"Where's Chip?" Eleanor was trying to gauge how much time she might have alone with her friend.

"I think he went out to lunch with some old buddies from high school. Knowing him, he will reappear right before we have soundcheck. He does this every time we play in Pittsburgh; I've just come to accept it." She motioned for Eleanor to sit on the couch. "Do you want some coffee, tea?"

Chip and Jenny always had the best-stocked bus.

"Tea is great, thanks!"

Jenny rummaged through her cupboards, prepping the tea.

"Hey, Jenny, can I ask you something?"

"Yeah, what's up?"

"Do you and Chip ever talk about having kids?"

"I mean, we've talked about it in the abstract, but it feels like something that is off in the distance. I don't think we will have kids anytime soon."

"What do you think would happen to you, like once you have a kid or get pregnant?"

"I don't know. I haven't thought it all the way through, yet; I guess I would just figure out how to be a mom."

"But like, what about your career . . . what happens to that?"

She thought for a minute.

"I don't know. I assumed that for me, having kids would mean I put things on pause for a while, career-wise. We could settle somewhere in the countryside and just take some time off. That's why it's still an abstract idea; I can't imagine a world where I am ready to check my coat."

"Check your coat?"

"Well, people say hang up your hat when you are retiring. I don't see a world where I retire, but when you check your coat, you do so with the intention that you will get it back."

Eleanor laughed.

"Why do you ask?"

"Okay, this stays between you and me, okay?"

Jenny nodded.

"Art and I had a fight today, after the interview."

"Wait, after he made a comment about you guys having a kid, what was that about? Like, have you guys talked about that before?"

"Literally, never. It was out of left field."

"Did you ask him about it?"

"Yeah, and it led to a fight. Like I asked why he had said that, and he basically told me that having a baby would be a good career move."

"What was his logic behind that one?"

"Well, he basically pulled the exposure card—that it would be good for his career to be seen as a good dad, and then it would be good for me to be associated with him. And I, in turn, could get press by being praised as being a good mother. The argument ended by him telling me how selfish I was and how I needed to be willing to check my coat, in your words, for the greater good of the band."

"How do you think he even got to a place where he was thinking about this?"

"I honestly have no idea. Like, I don't know why the thought of us having kids would ever have even crossed his mind."

"Okay, this might sound crazy, but bear with me for a second. Do you think that he possibly likes you? And he knows that if you have his kid, maybe you will start to like him, too. If nothing else, it would ensure that your lives are forever intertwined."

Eleanor felt a twinge of annoyance that this was the second time she had been asked this question today.

"Maybe this is his way of telling you that he likes you, without actually having to admit it." Jenny continued, "And, if he got angry, maybe it was his way of showing you that he cares."

Eleanor groaned. "I don't know how he could go from insulting me and barely being able to be around me to wanting to have children with me."

"I don't know . . . this is Art who we are talking about; he has always been the most difficult to read."

Before Eleanor could respond, Chip and a few of his friends stumbled through the door.

"I love Pittsburgh!" Chip declared, walking over and kissing his wife.

"Hey, it's Ellie Quinn!" said one of the guys who had followed in behind Chip.

He looked vaguely familiar. Eleanor was sure that they had had at least one class together in high school, and they had almost definitely been in the same middle school.

"Hey!" She said, ignoring the fact that she couldn't remember his name.

"I haven't seen you since Mrs. Herold's science class! How are you?"

"Oh, you know, just living the dream."

"I bet you are! We always knew that you were going to be someone."

"Did you? That's sweet. Well, I should probably go; thanks for the tea, Jenny."

The last thing she felt like doing was reliving high school days with someone whose name she couldn't even remember. She doubted that he had truly thought in high school that she was going to be someone. She had been quiet and kept to herself. It was a fluke that Jenny had found her and invited her to be a part of the band.

She paced the parking lot four more times before she reentered the arena. It was the earliest she ever had been to soundcheck.

17

October 18th

Cynthia

As soon as you called, I knew I had to come. There was no way I could know where you were and then not come to see you. Also, would you really have wanted me to ship a very expensive instrument via UPS?"

Jess and I were curled up on the couch with hot beverages: espresso for Jess and tea for me. Kristy was off to work, and I had a few hours to catch up before class.

"Are you sure you are not putting your life on hold to be here? I don't want to have to drag you into this chaos with me."

"What else are friends for than to haul themselves across the country to hand-deliver a guitar?"

"What reason did you give your team for your sudden urge to go to Seattle?" Jess was a talented pop star, the edgy kind that was featured on every song. Even at 7:00 a.m., her eyes were outlined heavily in kohl and mascara. Sometimes I wondered if she ever took it off.

"I am fulfilling my lifelong dream of finding Sasquatch."

I rolled my eyes dramatically.

"You know me; I have always loved a good conspiracy theory," she continued.

"Never in my life have I heard you ever utter the words Sasquatch or even Bigfoot."

"Okay, fine—I told them that I wanted some R and R before my next album starts recording. I had apparently heard of an excellent spa outside of Seattle. I also threw in something about how the mountains are supposed to be a helpful inspiration for writing music. I justified the last-minute trip by saying that the spa I wanted to go to only took really short notice reservations. Apparently, I had been trying to get in for months and was finally able to book an appointment."

"I love you. How long can you stay?"

"I don't have anything that I have to physically be in New York for until two weeks from now. So, I am here until you kick me out."

"Do you want to come to my show on Saturday?"

"Are you kidding me? That's half of the reason I'm here!"

"Okay, go with Kristy, but you have to find some way to disguise yourself. I'm serious!" I said as she started laughing. "I want to hide out for as long as I can."

Jess traced the floral pattern on her mug, distracted. "You know that he has called me a few times? Did I tell you that?"

"Wait, which he? Art, James, or Chip?" Chip seemed the most unlikely. He knew Jess, but I didn't think he had her phone number. I wouldn't put it past him to track it down and reach out to her to make sure I was okay.

Jess laughed. "All three, actually. Chip's call was my favorite. He was so awkward and Chip-like about the whole thing. He started off by saying, 'I am not sure if you have heard the news' as if he were worried that he would be the bearer of bad news. But his call was sweet; he just wanted to ask if I could pass on a hello from him if I heard from you. He said that he was worried and wanted to make sure that you were okay."

I teared up again; I missed him.

Jess took a deep breath. "But that isn't who I meant. James called me the night you ran away telling me what had happened and basically threatened me in an attempt to get your location out of me. At that point, I didn't know anything, and I told him that. I don't think he believed me. He even called my manager, trying to strong-arm us. I had been truthful about not knowing, though. I don't think your parents called me until a few days later. I think they wanted to try to ride out the storm a little first before calling. I had my legal team tell James that he was not allowed to call me again. I had never seen James act like that. He was scary. I see now why you didn't push back when he proposed the whole relationship thing in the first place."

I had never thought about the fact that I feared James. I knew that people joked about not wanting to be on his bad side, but I had always assumed that was something people said about management. I had never been on James's bad side, so I had no idea what that might be like. But, thinking back, I did try extra hard to remain in his good graces, as if I had subconsciously known.

"Oh, gosh, I am so sorry. You shouldn't have been caught in the crossfire like that. It was between James and me and the band. He should never have threatened you." I felt sick to my stomach.

She shrugged, "Eh, I can take it. I had always heard rumors that James had a mean side. Now I can say that I experienced it firsthand. Anyway, James' little power trip was, sadly, not the worst of it."

"Oh, gosh, no. Art?"

She nodded.

"Do I even want to know what he said?"

"He also called me the night you ran away. I think he thought you had come to my place or that I was sending my jet for you. He was also beyond drunk, which, I didn't expect any less from Art, but it was the most incoherent I had ever seen him. I think he was the first one who called me, and, at that point, I hadn't even seen that he had proposed. I started panicking because I had no idea what he had done to you. When he finally realized that I had no idea what he was going on about, he asked if I had been on Instagram or Twitter recently. I hung up on him because he was doing that narcissistic Art thing where he just expected me to know everything about him. But this time, it involved you, and I was so mad."

"Wait, you actually hung up on him?" Just the thought of hanging up on him made me feel a shiver of fear for Jess. I didn't want to consider what that meant about how much power Art had held over me.

"Yeah, I was fuming. He just assumed that I was waiting on pins and needles for the latest update. I don't live like that. If one of my friends wants me to know something, they will tell me. At that point, there was no reason for me to believe that you were in more danger than before. Seemed like the farther from Art you got, the safer you probably were."

"Sorry I didn't tell you that night. I was limiting my calls and texts because I was afraid of getting pinged."

Jess raised her perfectly manicured eyebrows. "Of getting what?"

"You know, pinged. Have you ever seen a spy movie? They're able to, like, track your location from cell phone signals. They ping your phone!"

Jess laughed, "I think you watch too much TV."

"Obviously not; it helped my grand escape."

"Fine. Anyway, I checked my phone. Obviously, it was like the first post on my feed. I saw what Art meant; he had proposed. So, then I got really angry and called him back." She smiled a dangerous smile.

I couldn't help but laugh. Jess was not someone I would want to mess with either. "What did you say?"

She examined her glossy black nails. "Basically, something along the lines of, 'what did you do . . . if you hurt her, I will find you and end you.'"

Something about my best friend threatening Art Bishop made me feel a little warm inside. "And what did he say?"

"He played dumb. Like he didn't understand why I wasn't on board with the whole thing."

"Of course he did."

"I know, I don't know why I was expecting something different."

"And I'm guessing you've heard from him recently?"

"Like to the point where I considered getting a restraining order. Art calls me all the time. I blocked his number, but he uses other people's cell phones or landlines. It's like he thinks I'm the only one connected to you. At the least, I'm the only one he is willing to bother five plus times a day."

"Okay, this might be a dumb question, but why do you think he cares so much where I am? It's clear to anyone who knew what was going on that he didn't love me, and I didn't love him. Yes, he proposed, publicly, and made sure there was no way I could say no. When I bolted, he lied and painted me as a crazy person. Why can't he just let it be and move on with his life?"

"I think he is worried about the story you would tell."

"What do you mean?"

"I mean, if you talk, there is no way he comes out looking good on the other end of this. You're clearly not crazy; you ran away because it was your only option to get out of an unsafe, unwanted relationship. You did what you needed to do to get out. You are a survivor. He is the abuser. I think he is trying to control the narrative."

Put so bluntly, I didn't know what to say. I could see Jess was right. Everything Art did was about controlling *his* image. He was constantly paranoid that it might suffer.

I broke the silence. "You know, he told me once that even if I did say something, no one would believe me, and it would just cause drama for him. He told me that he had a future, but I had none."

Jess pursed her lips, looking murderous again. "Why does that not surprise me?"

I smiled wryly. "I know, me neither, but the worst part of it was, I kind of believed him. Who am I apart from Kittanning? I started to believe the narrative that I wasn't enough to stand on my own two feet without the band."

She leaned over and hugged me. "You are enough. You are more than enough. You are *awesome*."

•◦⤜◦⤛◦•

I felt like I was a whole new person. Having Jess in town felt like my life was slowly going back to what it was meant to be, as if the pendulum was finally righting itself. We couldn't really do anything in public because that would be a clear clue as to where I was. Still, we were planning on ordering Thai takeout that night with Kristy after Gabe and I practiced.

"Wait, are you telling me there's a second runaway rock star that I need to protect?" Randy asked me on our way to Gabe's. He apparently had some shopping he needed to do in the area and didn't mind taking me to our impromptu band practice.

"No, I promise, nothing like that. Jess is cautious about leaving the house and going out; she doesn't want to alert anyone that I am here."

"Will she get the chance to meet your boyfriend before she jets off again?"

"He is not my boyfriend. We're simply friends; there is nothing more than that." Even if 'more than friends' sounded more tempting with every passing day.

"Mhmm."

"So, are you and Sandrine able to come on Saturday?" I had invited them both.

"Yeah, we wouldn't miss it. After all, it's not every day that you get to see a major celebrity perform for free."

"What are you talking about? I could perform for you for free every day—why didn't you ask? I could just serenade us on the way to class every morning!"

"But that would mean giving up our wonderful conversations; I could never do that!" he said sarcastically.

"Yeah, whatever." I couldn't help but smile. I would miss our conversations.

I felt ten feet tall walking into Gabe's apartment with my own guitar.

"Wow, you work fast!" he said, admiring it as I pulled it out of the case.

"I have connections," I teased. "But seriously, there was no way I was going to get up on stage and not have the guitar I love."

"Great, so if we bomb, we can't blame the guitar."

"You mean if *you* bomb; there is no way I am going to bomb with this baby," I said, pulling the guitar close to my chest.

"Whatever you need to tell yourself."

We ran through the songs we had picked out. It was different to do this all for the first time with someone new. It was unlike playing with Art or Jenny or Chip. I could read them without even trying; we had been playing together for so long. But this was new and exciting.

"Hey, I think my friend who works for the *Seattle Times* is going to be there. On Saturday," he mentioned, too casually.

"Really, why?"

"To hear you play."

"To hear *us* play," I corrected him.

"Yes, but I told her about you. You might not believe me, but you are crazy talented. You're good enough to have a record deal or at least consistent shows or something. So anyway, my friend writes for the *Times*, and I told her that it was just some open mic night, or whatever, but that she should come anyway and prepare to be mind-blown."

"I think you oversold me," I tried to laugh.

"No, I am serious. I believe in you." He was beaming with pride, believing that he was the one who had discovered me.

"I have always wanted to start a band." I left out the fact that I already sort of had.

"What do you want to do, like when you grow up or whatever. What is your big dream?"

"You tell me yours first, I need to think."

Gabe pushed his hands into his pockets and shrugged. "For me, it's easy. I want to be an accountant. I always have. I just really like numbers. I realize that might sound lame. Umm, I also want to bike across a country. And teach my kids how to play the fiddle because it is an under-appreciated but significant part of American history."

"Wait, go back. You want to bike across a country, like *this* country?"

"No, that's a little too ambitious. I would be fine with any country. I am really into cycling, and I think it would just be a cool brag to randomly drop the fact that I have biked across a country."

"Which country do you have in mind?"

"Well, Monaco is pretty small."

"Isn't it surrounded by mountains?"

"Yes, you raise a good point. I bet I could bike across Liechtenstein in a day."

"I think *I* could bike across Liechtenstein in a day."

"I would hope so. Okay, so you, now that you've had time to think, what is your big dream?"

"I mean, biking across Liechtenstein sounds pretty great."

"Hey, that's my dream!"

"Okay, fine. Honestly? You can't laugh," I gave my most serious expression.

"Hand on my heart." He mimicked putting his hand over his heart.

"I want to be a singer. But not in a band. No offense to our newly formed duo, but I want to just be El—" I paused. I wanted to just be Eleanor. But I couldn't tell him that. "I want to just be Cynthia. I want to be known for the things I create."

"You deserve credit for your work," he said it as if this was obvious.

"Thank you." I paused, trying to think about what to reveal next. "I write music, too. I would like to write lyrics for people."

"Wait, can we sing one of your songs on Saturday?"

I felt myself freeze. We would have to sing something I had written since leaving Kittanning. James or Art or someone had heard or read everything else I had written. It didn't feel safe or right to sing something I had written under the veil of Kittanning.

Then, almost against my will, my answer came out of my mouth: "Yes, let's do it."

"You know that means that I do probably need to get the music tonight, so I can practice."

"Oh, duh, sorry, um, do you have a pen? I left my notebook at home. Or you know what, can I play it for you first? Sometimes it is hard to tell how a song is just by the lyrics and chords."

"Yes, please!" He looked like a kid in a candy store. It was cute.

I picked up my guitar and started strumming. I realized that subconsciously, I started strumming the first chords to "Never Mine to Love" and quickly changed it to another pop song.

I sat down and slowly began to play my most recent piece. When I finished, Gabe was quiet. I didn't know how to read his silence.

"That was beautiful. Can I ask you something?" he said, sitting down next to me.

"Yeah, of course."

"Is that how it felt to be in an abusive relationship?"

I was going to cry, and it wouldn't be the first time. Gabe reached for some tissues.

"I mean, it matches what you told me a while back. I don't want to intrude; it's just that before, you told me how poorly he treated you. Now, I know how you felt." He put his hand on my shoulder.

"Yeah, he kind of turned me into a mess," I gestured at the crumpled tissue in my hand.

"Cynthia, I am so sorry. You're not a mess. You're an incredibly talented, courageous woman. I mean it."

"Thank you." I could tell he did.

18

April 11th

Eleanor

Eleanor hoped that Art's spontaneous interview comments would end once they left western Pennsylvania, but those hopes were quickly dashed. If he had a microphone, she could now bet on him making some sort of statement regarding the future of their relationship.

She didn't know what to do.

She had talked about it to James, who was absolutely no help at all. He pretended to be on her side while still justifying Art's behavior. He argued that it was good publicity. Why was it such a big deal? James didn't seem to grasp or care about the fact that it was her life that Art was planning. He brushed her off, saying that the news cycle changes all the time, promising that people would soon forget Art's comments.

Chip and Jenny had seemed to fall for this weird idea that Art actually liked her. Apparently, being a controlling jerk was his only way of expressing his love. Eleanor tried to confide in Jenny about how much she hated being in a relationship with Art. Jenny had been sympathetic; she wouldn't want to be in a relationship with him either. Maybe all this would phase out.

Jenny hadn't sided with Art, per se, but she definitely hadn't sided with Eleanor.

Eleanor felt trapped. Suffocated. And she couldn't tell the people she loved the most.

They had been on tour for a little over a month. The glamour was starting to wear off. For Art, sharing a bus with Ellie had also gotten old. For one thing, she snored. Sure, maybe this wasn't her fault, but it felt pretty personal at three o'clock in the morning.

The sentiment went both ways.

Art was trying his best to please Eleanor, to make her like him. But so far, all his efforts were coming up empty. He was trying to be kind to her. He was trying to compliment her in front of the camera. He talked about the life that he was planning for them. Most women would have considered this a turn-on. Here was a guy who cared about their future together: a man with a plan. But all this seemed to have the opposite effect on Eleanor. Instead, she just grew angrier with him. Most nights, she wouldn't even look at him at all once they got back to their bus.

But, Art reasoned, Eleanor was acting so selfishly. It was not like this had been all sunshine and rainbows for him. He spent so much time out of his day talking about Eleanor, praising her to different people, complimenting her. It was exhausting. He didn't want to do any of this.

And then there was the actual show he had to put on while they were on stage.

Usually, when they toured, Art knew how to work the crowd. He considered himself quite the ladies' man. But now, the whole arena knew that he was with Eleanor. Flirting with girls would not be to his advantage. Instead, he realized what made the crowd go wild was seeing the way he loved Eleanor. If he shared her mic, it was the loudest roar he had ever heard a crowd give. If he kissed her on stage, it was as if it were the world's most anticipated kiss.

Eleanor, for the most part, had realized this as well. She now had to spend a significant amount of energy on stage trying to figure out what Art would do next. Before their relationship, this had been easy for Eleanor. Art had been easy for her to read. But now, sharing the stage felt frightening and unpredictable. She never knew when he would say something to the crowd or make his way to show affection to her. The literal song and dance gave her severe anxiety. Just knowing that he might kiss her at any moment stole her sleep at night.

To be honest, she was not sure how she was supposed to act on stage, either. The crowd loved to see her and Art together, but she dreaded it. Performing had always felt like an extension of herself. She felt whole and at ease, as if it were something she had been born to do. Now, she just felt sloppy and confused. She knew well enough that she was supposed to lean into whatever Art was doing.

She wished that she were Jenny, protected by a drum set. No one would ever attempt to kiss a drummer mid-song.

Before the tour, James had held a special rehearsal for them, just so they could practice being a couple on stage. It had been awkward, to say the least. Both believed they were suffering more than the other. Singing as a couple looked so normal and natural when everyone else did it. Eleanor spent her time watching hours of tapes, as if she were an athlete, watching the way everyone else handled sharing the stage with their significant other. Each performance she watched, she noticed the couple performed better together than alone.

There was no amount of coaching or training or tape-watching that would ever get her and Art to this level. It was a hopeless task.

As the shows came and went, Art seemed to be trying to be more and more physical on stage. It was as if they were trying to convey that their relationship grew stronger the longer they toured together.

There could be nothing further from the truth.

No matter the disputes or tensions, the band gathered after each show to have a drink together and debrief. Depending on who had opened for them, the opener was also invited. It was a much-needed ritual to blow off whatever steam had accumulated during the previous twenty-four hours.

On this tour, these gatherings had become an impossible misery for Eleanor. Possibly the most frustrating thing about them was she couldn't even count on Art suffering, too. In fact, he seemed to be more and more eager for the band to hang out after the shows. It felt like he was rubbing this whole situation in her face.

He was not only controlling the narrative of her life, but he was enjoying himself while doing it. She felt sick.

In Atlanta, the crowds had been fantastic.

They had covered "I've Got a Woman" by Ray Charles. They always covered a song by an artist from the city where they were playing.

On their first tour, they had started this tradition to win the crowd over. Now, they performed out of pure love and respect for the artists who had walked the streets before them.

On this tour, Eleanor had done her best to avoid covering love songs: she didn't want to give Art another excuse to crowd her space. For the Atlanta show, she had suggested they sing "Hit the Road, Jack." She had been one hundred percent serious in her proposal, but she had also wanted to see Art and James's faces when she suggested it. Needless to say, her song selection was quickly vetoed.

Art had suggested, "Hallelujah, I Love Her So." Eleanor vetoed. She was not going to disrespect Ray Charles by singing that song with contempt in her heart.

She had felt okay singing "I've Got a Woman," in part because Kanye had turned it into a song about a gold digger. She had even convinced Jenny to use the beat of "Gold Digger" in their version. Eleanor argued that it would be a perfect balance of the two well-known songs.

And then, the cherry on top. When Eleanor was chatting with Chip before soundcheck, he casually mentioned that he was also a talented rapper. He never got to rap except in the shower. Jenny had heard him and vouched for his capabilities. That settled it; they would have him don a trucker hat and hoodie and rap the final verse of "Gold Digger" while the band sang the bridge of "I've Got a Woman."

It had turned out better than any of them had thought. Chip killed it, and the crowd ate it up. It was one of the few moments on stage during the tour that Eleanor forgot she was supposed to be in love with Art. She forgot that she would have to go back to a shared bus with him. She forgot she was supposed to be in love with him. Performing was fun again.

And then, in a cruel juxtaposition, the next song was "Home." They had been performing it acoustically. The stage set was simple: only two stools were brought onto the stage, one for Art and one for Eleanor. Backup dancers moved in a beautiful choreography that looked like they were serenading each other. Whenever she saw a clip of their performance, Eleanor always thought it looked romantic.

She and Art sang the whole song sitting on these stools angled toward each other. It made it look as if they were singing into each other's eyes. Typically, this was a painless moment, given Art's unpredictability on stage. They sat, and she kept an eye on him the whole time.

For some reason, tonight, only one stool made it onto the stage. There was no time to figure out a solution. One minute Eleanor was looking around, confused, the next, she was being swooped into Art's lap. And he held her there. Tightly. As if he was trying to say, you are mine; you are not going anywhere. At one point, she had tried to squirm her way out of his grasp, thinking this couldn't be comfortable for him either, but it was hopeless. He had her trapped.

There was no way he thought this looked natural. Never did someone over the age of five perform while sitting on someone's lap. It was the most ridiculous thing.

It wasn't that Art had hidden her stool from their crew, but he had moved one stool behind a prop backstage. If the crew had really been looking, the seat would have been found. But there was no time in the quick turnover between songs to find the misplaced stool.

He had known or at least been prepared for only one stool making it onto the stage that night. He had prayed that the seat belonging to Eleanor's side of the set would be the one that didn't appear.

Truthfully, he was mad about the way she had manipulated the Ray Charles song that night. It was a song about a man and a woman's love, and yet somehow, Chip and Eleanor sang more of it than him. She was the one who had scripted it. She should never be trusted to do that; James should have known better. When she was the one who divided out a song, he always got less singing time. Art was convinced this was purposeful.

On top of everything, she had the nerve to let Chip show off his rap skills on stage. He was a guitar player, a pawn, a background character. What had led her to believe that he should rap? She was lucky that hadn't backfired.

Finally, he had been robbed of the romantic moment of singing "Hallelujah, I Love Her So." That had always been one of his favorite Ray Charles songs. It would have been perfect, and the crowd would have gone crazy. It was as if she had set out to sabotage him on purpose. Everything she did was to spite him. He was sick of it.

So, he had hidden her stool. This was harmless in comparison to what she had put him through all day. Plus, he had to do something to prove that he was still in control, to show that he was still the one in charge.

By the time the show was over, Eleanor had almost forgotten the high she had felt after their "Gold Digger"/"I've Got a Woman" mashup. Everything had been clouded by "Home."

Art did everything he could to make sure the two of them were not alone between leaving the stage and walking to the room where James was waiting for them with a beer. He knew that if she had the chance, she was going to yell at him.

At this point, she was honestly too angry to yell at him.

Instead, she pulled Jenny to the side, holding back her tears, "Hey, can I sleep in your bus tonight? Is there space for me? I mean, I'll sleep on the couch."

"Yes, of course! What is wrong?"

Eleanor realized that in Jenny's mind, there was nothing wrong with what Art had done. For some reason, this made Eleanor shut down. She wasn't going to say anything about it if Jenny hadn't noticed; she didn't want to be known as a whistleblower. Ellie didn't want Jenny to think she was overreacting.

This gesture would have looked nice to an outsider: he provided a solution when her stool didn't appear. Otherwise, what would she have done? Awkwardly stood alone? She couldn't tell Jenny what was actually going on. She wouldn't understand. Maybe this was all in Eleanor's head anyway.

"I'm on my period, and I feel super weird about sharing a bathroom with Art. I mean, it is close quarters for us already, and I just can't do it," she lied.

"Oh yes, say no more! I'll tell Chip to move into your bus. Why don't you just plan to sleep on my bus the rest of the week."

Art was outraged. He knew for a fact that she was not on her period. What a weak excuse. As if he didn't track her period. She greatly underestimated him.

In the safety of Jenny's bus, Eleanor tried again to mention her current worries about Art.

"Do you think it was weird that he had me sit on his lap during the show tonight?"

"Weird, you mean from a visual point of view, or weird in that Art had you sit on his lap?"

"Both, I think."

"I mean, we can watch the tape back later and check what it looked like . . . I don't think it was the most normal thing he could have done, but I am sure that he thought it was just the polite thing to do. I bet that he was worried that if he didn't do something, you would be mad, you know? I bet he was trying to protect the crew."

"Yeah, I guess. But where was the other stool?"

"I don't know. It is honestly amazing that things don't go missing more often. I mean, there are so many moving parts to a tour. And we have so many set changes on this tour."

"That's true. I'll just double-check with the props manager to make sure that the second stool was found." Eleanor tried to convince herself that this was just a random fluke.

"Why don't you just have James do it? That is his job."

Eleanor didn't feel like she could trust James. She didn't really know why, but recently, he was changing. He stopped talking about the relationship as if it had an end date but as if it would last far further into the future than initially planned.

Eleanor couldn't tell Jenny that. She didn't want to be thought of as paranoid. Instead, she just agreed with Jenny and let the whole thing drop.

Before she went to bed, she checked her phone one last time. She had two unread messages.

The first was a message from James that he had sent to her and Art.

Again, great job tonight. And the whole thing with the stool, AMAZING. America loves you guys, keep it up!

This was not going to help the case that she was trying to build against Art.

The second was from Art.

You lied to sleep in Jenny's bus this week. You are so crazy about everything. Get over yourself. You are a manipulative liar. You're not as good of a performer as you think you are. You would have flopped up there without me tonight. Learn to be grateful.

She was sure that he was drunk. He only would put something like that in writing if he was drunk.

He usually was careful to only say something like that to her face when it would be her word versus his. Who did she think they would believe anyway? Art had once asked her that when she threatened to tell James about how he talked to her. He was right. She had no proof. And James wasn't going to ruin Art's career on something that was only hearsay.

Sometimes, he slipped up and sent her a text saying how he really felt. She always made sure to screenshot the messages. She was slowly building up her case against him. She knew that she would need to have some proof that he was as awful as she was claiming him to be.

The band had long since decided that they would limit their drinking while they were on tour. They didn't want to ruin their success by drinking or doing drugs. They had a beer together after the show, and usually, that was it. This was a lot easier of a pact to make than to keep. They had started touring when they were so young that the rule had felt natural. Eleanor knew that Art broke this rule. He stashed alcohol in their bus. She had suspected this for a long time, but she had never seen the evidence. This was the one advantage of sharing a bus with him.

She had also learned how much he drank.

She drank. It was not like she had some weird aversion to alcohol. But for Eleanor, this was more about breaking the pact with the band. Even if everyone was breaking this rule, she didn't want to let them down. She especially didn't want to end up as a washed-up singer whose career was ruined by alcohol.

But Art did more than drink. He would lie about how much he drank.

Once they had gone out on one of their forced dates, and Eleanor, who had gotten into this habit years ago, started counting his drinks. Throughout the evening, he had washed down over twelve drinks.

The morning after their night out, Kittanning had a meeting. He commented that he didn't feel great, which Eleanor joked was on account of having twelve drinks the night before.

She had never seen him so angry in front of other people. He called her a liar. He said he had never drunk that much in one sitting in his life, and she was trying to make him look bad. He didn't sleep well, which was why he had a headache. It had nothing to do with alcohol. Also, was she that crazy that she felt like she needed to count someone's drinks?

She had been stunned. She had no idea what she was supposed to say to that. She had been there. She had, like a crazy person—according to Art—counted his drinks. She was not his caretaker.

Why would she do that? Who did she think she was, some saint? Eleanor didn't know what to say. Her comment had been meant as an off-handed joke.

James had thankfully defused Art's rage by changing the subject. When they were alone in the car later that day, Art informed her that she was never allowed to talk about him like that again. She was an embarrassment. Did she not know how to talk to people? And she didn't need to be such a crazy person, counting his drinks. She needed to chill out.

She had been silent the whole ride to her apartment.

October 21ˢᵗ

Cynthia

I was not used to being this nervous before a show. Well, that was an exaggeration. I had always felt the nerves a little bit, but they were usually excitement and anticipation.

These nerves felt like the world was ending.

Maybe this was a good thing. Perhaps this was proof that I wasn't the person that I used to be? I tried to remember how I had felt before my first show. When we first started singing in bars in Pittsburgh, it felt awkward, and I would feel shaky, world-ending nerves before we would go on. I had felt like I was an imposter, like I didn't deserve to be on the stage. And then James had found us. Suddenly, I had justification for being there, for existing in the spotlight.

On our first tour, we had opened for another Pennsylvania native: Ben Reeves, who I had been listening to for years. I remembered that I was so star struck, I couldn't say more than two words the first time I met him.

If I really thought back, I felt more nervous than I usually would admit before our first show. We had been told, rather strictly, by James and by Art later, repeating James' words with his own aggressive twist, that this was our one shot. There was so much riding on our first album and our first tour. This was our make it or break it moment.

I don't think I ate for two days before our first show, I was so nervous.

The same message was repeated before our first headlining tour. There turned out to be a lot of make it or break it moments in those early years. I remember just waiting to do something to mess everything up for everyone. I lived in fear of being the one to be our downfall.

And then, suddenly, somewhere along the way, I stopped getting nervous in the same way. It was as if it had all become easy—old hat—and I no longer felt the same need to try all the time. People stopped threatening that we were on the verge of messing everything up. I had become someone who floated along. I realized that I had stopped trying because I didn't think I was going to fail.

But now, here I was again, fully aware of my own ability to fail.

J.K. Rowling, after the great success of *Harry Potter*, released her next book under a pseudonym. She wanted the book to be judged on its own merit. I felt the same way. I was going to prove that I was able to do this. It felt like I had to perform naked. This was who I was, raw and exposed, for the world to judge as they would—no pretty costuming, clout, or special effects to create an illusion of talent.

And there was a very high likelihood I would bomb. This would not only be an embarrassment to myself but to poor Gabe, who I had suddenly dragged down this path with me. Poor Gabe, who thought that he was setting me up for stardom when, in fact, I had spent the last month lying to him about the reason for the performance nerves I was feeling.

I realized I had nothing to do all day. That was another weird feeling. Usually, on the day of a show, I had to do something or be somewhere, which proved to be a great distraction from the night's events. This show was not nearly on the same level as what I had been doing for the last ten years, but there was still an ingrained need to be prepping something or rushing somewhere.

Jess had been sleeping on the couch and doing everything she could to make her visit to Seattle invisible. It was a weird but wonderful system we had developed.

Kristy was the only one of us who could freely come and go as she pleased. She was currently out getting takeout brunch for us.

Gabe and I had agreed to meet beforehand so we could drive together to the bar.

To be honest, I wasn't sure how big of a deal to make this night. Gabe had worked it out to be a big thing in his head because he had invited his friend from the paper. I was glad he was taking this seriously because then I could at least use that as my excuse for taking this so seriously. To be honest, I wasn't sure how to not take a show seriously. It felt counter to everything in me. The idea of that felt disrespectful to the audience. I could almost hear James's voice in my head reminding me of this.

But, I repeated to myself, this was just some random open mic night in West Seattle.

"So, how did you guys get a spot anyway?" Kristy asked when she returned with our brunch.

"What do you mean?"

"This bar is actually super well-known for live music. People try for months to get a spot there. Like, it's a huge deal that you got a spot—and on a Saturday, no less! Real musicians play at this bar. People with albums and record deals. They come back and play here as a tribute to Seattle."

"I *am* a real musician with albums, and I had a record deal," I said, a little too defensively.

"They don't know that. No offense, but no one knows who you are."

Come to think of it, I wasn't sure how Gabe got us a spot. Suddenly, I felt myself starting to panic. What if Gabe knew who I was, and this whole thing had been an elaborate setup? What if he had used my name to get a spot?

I texted him, asking, as casually as I could, how he had managed to get us into a well-known club on a Saturday night.

"Don't be mad," he responded. Then I watched for what felt like hours as the typing ellipses flickered across the screen. Finally, his next message came through: "Monica had taken a video of us singing karaoke at that bar a while ago. I showed my buddy who works at the bar to prove that you were good; we weren't messing around. And it worked. Sorry, I should have told you that there was a video."

I felt myself let out a sigh of relief.

"He had a video of us singing karaoke," I reported back to Jess and Kristy.

"Oh, good thought on his part!" Kristy said before taking a sip of her mimosa. "And who knows, maybe this will be your big break!" she added with a wink.

By the time Gabe picked me up that afternoon, I had reapplied deodorant three times. I was so agitated.

He gave me a kiss on the cheek. "Hey, you look like a rock star!"

"Wait, is this too much makeup?" I hadn't applied a full face of makeup in over a month. I barely recognized myself in the mirror.

"No, I meant it as a compliment; you look the part!"

"Oh! Yes, well then, thank you."

"Are you nervous?" he asked. I realized I hadn't spoken in a few blocks.

"Yeah, I guess, are you?"

"I mean, a little. But I also really don't mind being in front of a crowd. Here is my plan: if I feel like we are about to get booed off the stage, I will just start playing 'The Devil Went Down to Georgia,' which is always a crowd-pleaser." He looked over and winked.

"Great plan!" I laughed.

When we got to the bar, Gabe and I picked a table away from Kristy and Jess. I didn't want to be distracted by them. I was also feeling cautious about being spotted with Jess. However, when I saw her disguise, I had to admit that she looked unrecognizable.

Gone was the punk-rock Pakistani chick. Apparently, she could take off the eyeliner. Jess had on a ridiculously perfect blonde wig, tinted '90s glasses, high-waisted mom jeans, a pair of Birkenstocks, and a faded Washington State t-shirt. She was industriously chomping away on a piece of gum. She looked exactly like she belonged in Seattle in the nineties.

I noticed Gabe's friends from the karaoke night came in twenty minutes before we were scheduled to go on. They recognized Kristy and pulled up chairs next to her. I prayed that none of them would look too carefully at Jess.

I heard our names being called, and slowly, we made our way to the stage, instruments in tow.

What happened next felt like flying. I had forgotten the freedom that came with being in the spotlight. I forgot about Cynthia, Eleanor, Kittanning, and Art. I remembered who I was and who I had been created to be. It was kind of like flying.

Our final song was the one I had written.

"Hey, everyone! It has been such a joy to share this room with you guys tonight. Before we head off for the night, I wanted to share with you guys a more personal song, something that I wrote myself, so please listen with grace." I smiled at the crowd. They were oddly warm and welcoming. I had forgotten how nice it was to play in a smaller venue.

The song was powerful. I had written it to be accompanied by a full band, but even stripped down to me and my guitar, I could feel the momentum as the song built to its climax. My voice reached out with boldness and confidence, not a trace of self-doubt as I enunciated every word. As I poured my full heart into the last line, something inside was unlocked.

As soon as I had strummed the last chord, I looked out at their smiling faces, glowing with what looked like pride. I let out a long breath. This was where I was supposed to be.

When we finally left the stage, I could tell that I was crying. I was bursting with joy.

"Hey, Rebecca!" Gabe said, motioning someone over to where we were standing next to the stage stairs. I needed a minute to come back to reality before going over to the table of our friends.

As soon as I saw her, my heart sank. I knew Rebecca Davis. Or at least, I had seen her. She had interviewed us the last time we were in Seattle. I remembered her for her intimidating stare. One that looked like it was going to peer into the depths of your soul. But, to her credit, she was one of the only reporters that Art had not tried to mess with, so her intimidating gaze must have worked to ward him away.

"Hey, Gabe and . . . Cynthia, is it?"

She knew. I could tell by the look on her face. Her eyes really were the window to her soul.

"Yes, hi, Rebecca! Nice to meet you!" I tried to stay calm.

"You guys were great, but Cynthia, you are something else. No offense, Gabe."

"None taken; she's the talent. I am just the man with a fiddle."

I didn't know what to do with the way he spoke with pride, hugging me against his side with a wide smile. He did nothing to take credit, and my heart took another jump of hope. I shook my head clear and refocused on the danger in front of me.

"So, Cynthia, are you from Seattle? I would love to sit down with you for an interview."

"I mean, I live here now, but I am not from here."

"Sadly, Rebecca, she is from Pittsburgh. Being a Steelers fan is her biggest flaw," Gabe teased, unaware of my growing discomfort.

"Interesting, Pittsburgh," Rebecca mused, almost to herself. "There is a really great music scene coming out of Pittsburgh." She added nonchalantly.

I could feel my face going red.

"Oh, is there? I mean, I think Seattle is better known for its musicians. I mean, Jimi Hendrix, Pearl Jam, Foo Fighters, Macklemore. I could go on." I couldn't, actually; those were all the Seattle musicians I could think of.

"Yes, Seattle has some great talent. So, just really quickly, I know you are probably wanting to go see your friends, but I have to ask: Did you come to Seattle to pursue a career in music?" Rebecca fixed those ice blue eyes on me and waited.

"Actually, no. I came here to go to school. Music has always just been a hobby. I mean, I would not be opposed to a career in music if there was an opportunity."

Her smile didn't quite reach her eyes. "That is a really nice guitar for a student who just plays as a hobby. Well, I will make sure to get your number from Gabe, and I would love to sit down and interview you both!" She looked only at me as she said this.

"Are you free on Monday? Cynthia and I have class on Monday together, and we could meet you afterward." Gabe was as excited as a puppy with a bone.

"I'll put it on my calendar."

And just like that, I could feel freedom slipping away.

I was well and truly rattled by the time we got to the table.

"Who were you guys talking to?" Jess asked as soon as we sat down, "I'm Mary, by the way." She extended her hand to Gabe and shot me a look.

"Hey, I'm Gabe. Have we met before?"

"No, I don't think so; I am just in town from Los Angeles visiting my cousins!" I had to laugh at the backstory she had created.

"Umm, that was someone Gabe knows from a paper here in Seattle. Rebecca Davis." I tried to hint at the impending danger.

"Hm, I see." Jess and Kristy said in unison, alarm crossing both of their faces.

"She wants to interview Cynthia," Gabe beamed. "She kept going on about how talented she is."

Both Kristy and Jess shot me panicked looks.

"Wow, what a lucky break," Kristy said dryly. I could tell she was being sarcastic.

"So, what did you think of the set?" I asked, trying to change the subject.

"Man, you really can sing!" Joe said, looking at me.

"I mean, the fiddle is cool, too," someone else added.

There was a round of encouraging agreements.

"Well, I want a beer," I declared and made my way to the bar, my head spinning with the events of the last thirty minutes.

Jess walked up to the bar with me, still chewing her gum obnoxiously.

"Okay, that last song that you guys sang, did you write it recently?"

"Yeah. I wrote it right after Art's interview. It's weird playing new material without it being vetting and critiqued by like eighty-seven people at the label, James, and the rest of the band."

Jess leaned in so I could hear her over the din of the bar, "E, I am telling you, it might be my favorite song that you have ever written. I'm not just saying that to feed your ego or because you're finally doing this on your own. Objectively speaking, I think it's your best yet. I mean, it was just so raw. The melody, the lyrics, the way you sang with all your heart . . . you brought people into the pain with you. I don't know—I wanted justice for you just listening to it."

"Really, promise me, writer to writer, that you actually liked it."

"I can't tell you how powerful that song is. You need to get it out into the world. I believe in you. And more importantly, I believe you. The world should hear your side of this story." Behind those ugly, tinted glasses, I could see the truth in her eyes. She really believed in me.

August 20th

Eleanor

Eleanor checked the tour schedule. They were in Salt Lake today, and then they would be in Denver, down to Dallas, and then they would have a break. She was counting down the moments until she could have a break. She needed to have a little bit of time away if she would make it the rest of the tour. She felt like she was on edge all the time, dangerously close to her tipping point. James had even offered anti-anxiety medication to help her cope.

She was planning on going to Pennsylvania to visit her family. She missed her family. They hadn't been able to come to as many shows as they usually would have. This year had been crazier than usual, and her family had a life outside of her tour schedule. Adam and his wife had come to the show in Pittsburgh, and they would meet her in Seattle. This would be a bonus. She had a cousin, Kristy, in Seattle who she would also get to see.

She needed to figure out a way to get through the next three shows. They were covering a Neon Trees song tonight. Jenny had always loved the Neon Trees because their drummer was also a woman.

She had never had any strong feelings either way about playing in Salt Lake.

As luck would have it, in the shows after Atlanta, the second stool didn't make an appearance during "Home." Three or four performances without the second stool, James was convinced that it looked more romantic with only one and cut it from the prop list. He ignored Eleanor's complaints.

Art had gotten worse as well. Since she had bunked with Jenny, he was extra sweet when they were in front of people, and then as soon as they were alone, he would yell and scream about any random thing she had done that day that pissed him off.

She was selfish.

She was crazy.

She was full of herself.

She was prideful.

She was an awful dancer.

She was a boring performer.

She was awkward.

She wasn't talented.

She was too emotional.

She was unable to sing on key.

She was ugly.

She was unable to do anything on her own.

She wasn't enough.

He said these things so often that she had started to believe them. It was hard not to. During her week staying with Jenny, he had stored up all of the hateful things he wanted to say. Now that she was in their shared bus again, he didn't hold anything back.

She couldn't escape the dread she felt when she thought about sharing a stage with him. She had a pit in her stomach each time she walked to their shared bus.

But mostly, she felt isolated.

⁘⸰᠃⸱⸰᠃

"They won't believe you," He had told her last night, once they were alone. She was sitting at the mini table, eating takeout. She had expected something. Art had overheard that she was planning on spending time with her family during the tour break.

"What do you mean?" She had learned how to have a conversation with this version of Art. She asked questions, never spoke in the definite unless she was sure of her response, and she no longer assumed she knew what he was talking about.

He walked over. "I mean if you mention to your family that you are unhappy in this relationship. There is no way they are going to believe you."

"I wasn't planning on saying anything to them." She could mentally feel herself shutting down. She made herself smaller, less threatening.

He sneered and leaned close, "You better not; I don't think you really realize how much of your future is in my hands. I am the one who has a future here. I am the one who has something to lose. Just because you aren't happy doesn't mean that the whole world needs to suffer with you."

"I am not going to say anything." She tried to sound sincere.

"I know you won't. I will make sure of it," he threatened her. They both knew he was threatening her; there was no need to point it out.

She sat in silence. Willing her mind to be anywhere but there. She tried to force herself to take up less space. As if somehow, this would make everything a little better, more manageable.

Two more shows. Eleanor just needed to make it through two more shows, and then she could have a break.

October 23rd

Cynthia

Monday came quicker than ever. I had spent all yesterday willing myself to think of anything other than my upcoming interview with Rebecca Davis. I couldn't take my mind off it.

On the car ride to school that morning, I told Randy about the situation I had gotten myself into.

"Maybe she just wants to interview you because you were good. I mean, I was there. You are good." He was clearly trying to make me feel better.

"I don't think so. The whole time she was talking to me, it felt like there was an agenda."

"Maybe she just wants to be able to claim that she was the journalist who discovered you?"

"Mhmm, maybe." But I doubted that. Rebecca knew who I was, and she wanted to be the journalist that outed me.

After class, Gabe and I walked, more quickly than I would have preferred, to the off-campus Starbucks where we were meeting Rebecca. The Starbucks was two floors, and Rebecca was waiting for us upstairs, where it was quieter. Large windows were designed to let in the light, but right now, it just felt moody and dark. Big, fat drops of rain poured down the glass like tears. I could feel myself shaking as I walked up the stairs.

Gabe took my hand and pulled me to a stop. "Are you okay?" he asked under his breath.

"Yeah, just tired," I tried to assure him as much as myself.

Once we found Rebecca and set our bags down, Gabe offered to get my drink, leaving me alone with her. She was even more intimidating than I remembered. Her gaze never left mine. It was clear that she was not intimidated by me. Her face seemed to be almost frozen into a permanent frown. I willed myself not to be the one to break the silence. I tried to remember how long the line downstairs was and calculate how long I would have to be alone with her before Gabe made it back with our coffees.

Rebecca leaned forward, putting her elbows on her knees.

"I know you," she said.

"Yeah, we met on Saturday night." I tried to play dumb, but my heart was in my throat.

Rebecca narrowed her eyes. "No, I mean, I know that you are actually Eleanor Quinn." She paused. I hadn't expected her to be so blunt. Maybe she was also calculating how long she would have me alone. I said nothing, so she continued, "I had suspicions as soon as Gabe sent me that video. I had to come and confirm for myself. I did some digging; I know that you have a cousin who lives in Seattle, and there was a woman in the crowd on Saturday who looked suspiciously like your friend Jess under that '90s getup."

I didn't know what to say. I could feel grief and despair washing over me.

"What do you want?" I asked, matching her position, putting my elbows on my knees.

"I want to help you."

My elbows slipped off my knees. I was stunned.

"Wait, you want to what?"

"It's no secret that Art Bishop has a bad reputation. And as journalists, we talk about these things. I know a woman who works for a paper in LA. When she interviewed him, he forced her into a room alone with him and tried to . . . you know. Every interview I've done with him, I have gone out of my way to avoid being alone with him. It's obvious how he treats the women around him." She shrugged as if the truth was simple and obvious. "Art Bishop is a nasty guy: that is a well-known, unspoken fact shared by every female who has ever met him." The intense stare was back. "I want to share your story. If you agree to tell it, I know there are journalists who will back you up. I am assuming that you wrote the last song you sang on Saturday about him?"

I nodded weakly. I was still too stunned to speak. Other people knew about the way Art acted. I wasn't the only one.

Rebecca Davis gave me a surprisingly warm smile. "I believe you, Eleanor. I want your story to be shared, that is, if you are willing to trust me with it."

I was trying to hold back my tears.

"You believe me?" I finally managed.

She leaned over and handed me a tissue. "Yes."

"Do you have a plan?"

"Yes. Does Gabe know who you actually are?"

"No, he really thinks my name is Cynthia, and I moved here from Pittsburgh."

"Do you want to tell him?"

I thought for a minute. "I do, but I don't think I'm ready today."

"That's fine. In that case, here is what we are going to do. We will have a fake interview now to keep your story going for your friend's sake. We will talk about this new talent that I have stumbled upon. When you can and want to, we can meet at my office or another place where you feel safe, and I can walk you through my plan. I can promise you this: this is your story to tell, and I will only share as much or as little as you feel comfortable with. Nothing is off the table, but nothing is required. If you decide you don't want me to run the story in a week, I will pull it—no questions asked. This is your story, not mine. It's not worth me ruining your life so I can run an article. You make the call, okay?"

"Can you meet me tomorrow? At my cousin's apartment where I have been staying? I will have someone draw up some paperwork, if that is okay with you, just to be safe."

"Yes, of course. I will sign whatever you want. I want to respect you."

That was what I had been waiting years to hear. Someone respected me. But more than that, someone believed me.

"Come by tomorrow, and I will tell you everything." I scribbled down the address and slid it across the table right as Gabe walked up the stairs, two iced lattes in hand, looking like this was the best day of his life.

To be honest, it was quite possibly the best day of mine.

Someone believed me.

·c⌒ᴗ°ːᴄᴄ⌐⌒ᴐ·

Rebecca showed up at precisely 2:00 p.m. Jess was there as a witness; she and her lawyer had helped me come up with some paperwork. I wanted to be sure that there was no way Ms. Davis could manipulate my words. I trusted her, but I wasn't taking chances; this was too important to me.

She read it over and happily signed everything, just like she had promised.

"Okay," I said, after everything was signed, "what's your plan?"

"Well, I just want to say right off the bat that I know that this is not a little thing. So, if anywhere along the way you don't feel comfortable, just tell me, and we will reverse or re-strategize."

I nodded. The more Rebecca talked, the more I liked and trusted her. She had the type of no-nonsense, take-charge personality that instantly made me feel safe. At the same time, I could tell that she took her job seriously and was not messing around.

"So, I want to first just hear your story all the way through, on the record. I am planning on everything being on the record if that is okay."

I nodded.

"And then I'll write the piece that will run in the *Seattle Times*."

This didn't seem as dramatic as I had thought.

"Okay, that works." I was very underwhelmed.

"Great, I am glad that you are with me so far. So, Kittanning is going to be playing in Seattle in a week and a half. I would like to run the story a few days before. With the *Times*, we have connections with a national morning show, and I think it would be compelling for you to do an interview the morning before they

211

play in Seattle." She took a breath. I could tell she was trying to gauge my reaction.

"I love it." I could feel my brain coming alive with ideas. "I just have one thing to add. I want to do a concert the night after their show. I know that is a lot to plan, but I'll make some calls. If it works, I want to announce that I am doing a show, in the article or on-air, whatever you think will reach more people, and I want to give the tickets away for free. I just want to see if people will come." I added the last bit meekly. I still doubted I could do this on my own.

"Done." She pulled out a recorder. "Eleanor Quinn, where do you want to begin?"

For the first time in my life, I sat down and told the whole story.

I talked about going to high school. I spoke about how Art had dated my sister, and somewhere along the way, my sister and I had lost our relationship. I told her how Kittanning had been formed. And then, finally, I told her about being forced into a relationship with Art. I held nothing back. I told her that it had all been a scam. I even explained James's role in the whole thing. The more I thought about it, the more I realized that James had done nothing to save me from a situation that he knew put me in distress.

•ᴄ⁓ᴆᵒₒᶜᴳ⁓ᵓ•

"Wait, so you are saying that James and his team had you go through all of that so the band would sell more records?" Rebecca had been mostly silent through my whole monologue.

"Yeah, I guess you are right. I don't think anyone meant for it to turn out that way. It started with the song 'Home.' The label wanted me to write a slower duet to sing with Art; they thought it would round out our album. James quickly realized that the rumors of us dating were helping the pre-sales for the album. From there, everything just exploded. I didn't really have a choice. We were literally just told one morning, you two are dating now. And from there, things escalated."

"You don't think that the label had you write that song to set off this whole chain of events?"

This question threw me off. I had never thought about this being something premeditated. I had thought it had just happened organically. But the more I thought about it, the more this made sense. The whole thing had been intended to lead up to Art and I dating.

I paused for a long time before I could answer.

"I honestly never thought about that. I guess I have always given everyone, especially James, the benefit of the doubt. Most of my energy has been spent blaming Art for how he handled things."

"What do you mean by that?"

"Art and I had very different ideas of what this relationship was going to look like. He thought that we should act as if we were an actual couple all of the time. He tried to make this relationship include everything that a normal couple would do, *even in private*. I refused, and I wouldn't budge. He never really got over that. I think he started to notice that the relationship was giving him a lot of good press, so he pushed me harder. He would say things in interviews that were totally off the book and unscripted, but I was supposed to just nod along. I had to act like I was just as in love with him, or else."

"Or else what?"

"James and Art had made it perfectly clear to me that if I did anything to put the relationship in jeopardy, my career would suffer. I would suffer."

"I am so sorry, Eleanor." I could tell that she meant it.

Finally, I had to tell her about the night in Denver. This was the part that I was most worried about sharing. The night had really been marketed to look like the world's best proposal. This was the proposal every girl dreamed of, right? I felt like I was crushing the world's dreams if I let people know it had actually been a nightmare. I had done everything I could to repress the memories of that terrible night. I didn't feel like I could escape.

"And then," I said with a sigh of relief, feeling physically lighter after sharing what had happened, "I got on a bus and ended up in Seattle. I knew that this would be a safe place to start over."

"What does starting over mean to you?"

"In recent years, the narrative that I am not good enough or talented enough on my own has been repeated to me over and over again. Music is the thing I love more than anything in the world. Starting over looks like me walking away from Kittanning. This does not mean I am ready to walk away from music. In fact, I aim to do the opposite; I want to make it as a solo artist."

"Can I ask about the song I heard you play last Saturday night? It was beautiful. Was that song about this experience with Art?"

"Thank you. Yeah, that is probably the most personal song I have ever written. It's called "Wasn't Love," and it was basically me walking through the grief that came with this whole 'relationship' with Art."

"That was one of the most powerful songs about an abusive relationship I have ever heard. My heart broke for what you experienced."

"Thank you." I took a breath. "If I am honest, for so long, I felt so alone and so scared about what my life was becoming. The best way to describe my relationship with Art is 'isolating.' I could tell people what was going on but not the whole truth. I couldn't do anything to jeopardize the band. Not even my closest friends really knew everything that went on. It got to a point where I didn't think anyone would believe me. Which was another lie that I was fed all over again."

"By who?"

"By Art. He claimed he was the one who had the power; he was the one who people would believe. He told me the world would see right through my emotional crazy."

"Thank you for the bravery it took to share with me."

"Thank you for believing me; it is the biggest gift I have ever received."

August 23rd

Eleanor

One more show. Eleanor just needed to make it through one more night.

James had pulled her aside the night before to tell her to be careful with her week off.

"What do you mean, be careful? I'm just going to visit my family."

James lowered his voice and said, "I mean that you need to be careful about what you say. You don't want to do something to ruin what you and Art have."

I frowned. "'What we have,' meaning this sham of a relationship?"

"'What you have' meaning something that is greatly helping both of your careers."

Eleanor ran her hands through her hair, exasperated. "James, this is helping the career of the band. This is not helping me personally." She was tired of being lumped in with the band. She shook her head, turning to walk away.

James grabbed her arm and jerked her back to face him. Never in her life had James laid a hand on her. She looked at his hand and then looked at him, horrified. He didn't release her.

"Eleanor, stop being selfish," he ground through his teeth. "I *need* you to get it through that pretty little head that you and Art's relationship is a good thing for the band and, therefore, a good thing for *you*. And yes, it is a great thing for Art. Why does that matter so much to you? Why can't you just get over yourself? Being connected to him is a good thing for you. Do you actually want to try to make it on your own?" James laughed in a mean way, and Eleanor recoiled. "Do you actually think you *could* make it on your own? I have known you since you were like what, sixteen? I don't think you understand what I have done for your career. The road goes both ways here."

He finally released her arm. She didn't know what to say. If she started talking, she was sure to cry. She wouldn't give him the satisfaction of seeing her cry.

She had heard that James Porzio had a dark side. People said that the best thing someone could do for their career was to stay on his good side. She could tell that she was dangerously close to the edge. For the first time in her career, in her life, she was challenging the system.

She knew that she should feel empowered. She had finally spoken up for herself. Instead, she just felt small and scared and even more isolated.

"Really, now you don't have anything to say?" James challenged her. "It's not the end of the world for you to give up a little of your precious comfort for the greater good."

She could feel something inside of her snap. He thought that this was such a big deal to her because she was a little uncomfortable?

"Give up a little of my comfort? James, you have made me put my life on hold for this charade. I am trying to tell you that I don't feel comfortable with where this is going. Art is out of control," she pleaded.

James spoke slowly, emphasizing each word, "And I am telling you that you need to let it go. I am serious. Watch what you say next week. Don't forget that *I* decide your future."

With that, he stalked away.

James was fed up with self-centered little divas. He didn't understand what the big deal was. She was getting to live the dream of so many people. Did she not understand how many people would kill to have her life? Yet, she was so ungrateful. She wasn't willing to give up a little of her freedom for the greater good. It wasn't just Art whose career she was helping. Good press for the band was also good for him and for everyone who worked for them. If she did something stupid or irrational, that choice would affect more than just Art and Eleanor. She ran the risk of damaging the jobs of hundreds of people who worked for her, yet she refused to see beyond herself.

He had faithfully stood by her side for years. And yes, she was talented. But everyone who made it thought they were better than they actually were. He was the one who had put his whole life at risk to try to make something out of this little band of teenagers from western Pennsylvania. He had bet right, thankfully, but there had been a considerable risk that the whole thing could have flopped. When Art's dad had called him all those years ago, he had gone as a personal favor. It was sheer luck the band was so good. He had been pressured by Art's dad to sign them.

Pressured was the wrong word. Mr. Bishop had blackmailed him, threatening James's career and reputation. And the threat had worked. It forced him to clean up his life. He had made some choices in his younger years that he wasn't proud of—choices Art's dad had found out about somehow.

He hoped that threatening Eleanor would motivate her to make some lifestyle changes, too.

It was odd to James that the most trouble on this tour had been caused by Eleanor. Usually, she was the easiest of them all. She was just happy to be there. Everyone knew that being on tour was her favorite part of her job. But something was different this time around.

James refused to believe that all of this was caused because she had to pretend to date Art. That might have been a small part of it, but how hard could this actually be on her? Every single woman in America under twenty-five wanted to date Art.

From James's perspective, this relationship was the best thing that had ever happened to the band. Art was being more attentive. He rarely showed up hungover to meetings. And they never had to worry about him bringing random girls home. It was a PR dream come true.

It seemed that even Jenny and Chip had come to accept and love the new relationship. James figured that it was a relief to them to not be the only couple in the group. It made the overall dynamic so much better. Jenny had even slowly stopped mentioning

ABBA. This was a first for her; usually, she wouldn't shut up about her Swedish nightmare.

The only person who seemed to be digging her heels in was Eleanor.

James knew what Art had planned for the next night. He had not really given his stamp of approval, but he had also not done anything to stop it. He couldn't stop thinking about how much of a win this would be for the band, for the tour. This tour would go down as one of the most iconic tours in history. His name would be attached to something historical.

Which was all fine and good, except for the fact that Eleanor had become a drama queen.

James knew celebrities were selfish; he had known this when he signed up for this job. When someone got famous so young, they had no idea what the real world was like; they had everything handed to them. Mostly he gave them a lot of grace. They did have to live their lives in the spotlight. But the way Eleanor was acting was the final straw. It was just over the top.

Sure, he wouldn't want his daughter dating Art. But sometimes you just had to make sacrifices for your job.

In the days that followed, James couldn't stop thinking about Art's planned proposal.

He had been reluctant at first. What if Eleanor said no? She was getting more headstrong by the minute. James had realized they could stage it in a way where she had no choice. They would cut her mic, just to be extra cautious. James didn't feel worried. For years, she had been trained how to act on a stage or in an interview. "Yes, and." You never negate what the person is saying. Instinctively, she would have to say yes while on stage. The conversation that she and Art had afterward would be their business.

James had to admit the way Art had set the whole thing up was quite genius. On top of that, it sounded like something Eleanor would love . . . if it were anyone but Art proposing.

James felt oddly calm about the whole thing. Art had really taken care of all the logistics.

Tonight, in his anger, he had almost told her that it was coming. Not as a warning but more as a threat. But there was a small part of James that was fighting back for Eleanor. He did love her and wanted the best for her. But he wanted the best for the band and, mostly, the best for himself.

His brain was being tugged in multiple directions.

But when it came down to it, there was no denying that Eleanor needed to get over herself and take one for the team. This proposal, if nothing else, would put them all down in the hall of fame. She had to recognize the power of that.

When they arrived in Denver, everyone seemed a little bit off to Eleanor. Jenny seemed a little extra giddy. Chip kept pulling Art aside to talk with him. James kept giving her contradicting and pained expressions. They all needed a break from each other; that was clear.

It was like the air between them had grown stale, but the hope of the coming break was livening things up again.

Earlier in the day, Jenny had looked at Eleanor and just burst into tears. That was a lot of emotion, even coming from Jenny.

"What is going on with everyone?" Eleanor finally asked Jenny when she got a moment alone with her. "Wait, oh my gosh, are you pregnant?" Eleanor felt a surge of joy. That would explain a lot.

"Oh my goodness, no, I am not pregnant. I'm just in a good mood. I like playing in Denver."

"Really?" Eleanor frowned; she'd never really thought twice about playing here.

"Yeah, and I like the set tonight. I'm pretty excited to cover 'Ho, Hey.'"

"Yeah, me too, I guess. Mostly, I'm ready for a break. I am excited about the next two shows but just because they're steppingstones to the break," Eleanor told her honestly.

"Really? You don't think there is anything big on the horizon for this show or the next?" Jenny was never good at being subtle, but she had been proud at this attempt. Later, Eleanor would look back and realize this conversation should have clued her in on the fact that Art was going to do something. She may have never guessed it would be a proposal, but she would have had her guard up.

"I mean, I don't think so. Do you have people you know at the show tonight?" Eleanor was trying to still figure out the reason for her peppy mood.

"No, I don't think I have anyone coming for a while. I have a couple of friends who moved to the West Coast who are going to come to those shows, but I don't think I know anyone in Denver."

Eleanor decided to let it go. Maybe Jenny was just in a good mood because she was simply enjoying the tour. It really shouldn't have been that big of a deal for her friend to be extra joyful.

But, of course, it *was* a big deal. Everyone was on edge, either in a good or bad way, about the upcoming proposal. Looking back, Eleanor would remember the way everyone backstage looked at her—with an extra glimmer of hope, anticipation, and excitement. She would remember how, right before she went on for the first song, James pulled her aside to tell her that no matter what, he really did want what was best for her. Jenny was in extra high spirits each time she saw Eleanor and Art interacting. And she would remember how Art ignored her, even more than usual.

The rest had dissolved into a blur of shiny lights and confusion.

October 27th

Cynthia

I paced around the living room so much that Kristy joked I would wear a hole in her floor.

I couldn't help it.

I didn't know if I was excited or nervous and scared. Most likely a mixture.

This feeling of nervousness was unlike any that I had experienced before. It was blended with anticipation and full-on fear.

The article was going to run tomorrow. The interview had been set up, very covertly, I might add, with *Good Morning America*. The whole thing had happened so fast but in slow motion at the same time. I still had a hard time believing this was happening.

The whole process had been hushed. Rebecca had a small team, mostly women, who worked with us to make sure everything was going according to plan. I had a sneaking suspicion that Art had hurt each of these women in one way or another. They were all sympathetic and respectful. Most of all, they all believed me.

Everything was set up so that James and Art would have no idea what was coming.

In a way, I wanted James and Art to experience the feeling I had suffered through on that stage, the whole world watching me get blindsided.

I didn't want them to be prepared with their counterattack before I even had time to strike.

This whole thing made me feel like a spy. It was both liberating and nauseating.

Today, I had another battle to fight. Today was the day I was going to tell Gabe.

Unofficially, this was going to be my last day of classes. There was no way that I could go back after the story ran. And I wasn't sure if I wanted to.

I had learned that writing the next great American novel wasn't what I wanted to do.

There was no way I was going to let Gabe find out the truth from a newspaper. If it hadn't been for him, I never would have found Rebecca in the first place.

This morning, I was also suffering from a case of graduation goggles. Looking back, I realized how much I was going to miss the routine that had developed. I would miss my drives with Randy, although he was going to stay on my staff. I also thought Randy might miss taking the class. He told me he had found it surprisingly interesting.

Gabe and I were going out after class. I had felt bold the night before, asking if he was free. I don't know why I had been so nervous waiting for his reply. We were just planning to grab ice cream at Molly Moon's, a local hot-spot famous for its wide variety of locally sourced seasonal flavors.

So much had happened since my interview with Rebecca Davis; it was hard to believe that it had been just a week ago. But really, that was how things had felt since leaving Kittanning. Time had become blurry, and the days seemed to move in fast-forward and slow motion at the same time.

We traveled in comfortable silence after class. It was sunny, for once, and we were both enjoying the beautiful weather. I don't think Gabe noticed me silently saying goodbye to the campus. It all felt surreal.

After traversing the better part of downtown Seattle, I had built up an appetite. We got our ice cream—honey lavender for me, cold brew for Gabe—and walked around the block to Kerry Park while we ate. It was tiny, but the view of Seattle was breathtaking.

I paused, unsure how to start this conversation.

"Okay, so I have to tell you about this woman I saw on the bus today," Gabe started as soon as we had sat down on the only free bench. I could tell he was going to launch into a story, but there was no way I would be able to pay attention.

"Wait, I have to tell you something," I interrupted. I couldn't help but cringe; I hated when people interrupted. I didn't wait for him to respond, though. "I need to tell you about why I moved to Seattle."

Confusion washed over his face. I had already told him a few details of why I had moved, and I could tell that he was trying to calculate what the missing piece of my story might be.

"Okay." The word came out more like a question.

I fidgeted with the mini spoon. "I know this is going to sound really weird. I've been trying to figure out how to tell you this for a while now. There's just no way to say this without sounding incredibly bizarre."

His look grew more confused. I could tell my ambiguity was helping no one.

I took a deep breath and plunged on. "Before I moved to Seattle, I was a singer, an actual singer—like, that was my full-time job. My real name is Eleanor Quinn, and I was in the band Kittanning." I looked down at my ice cream to avoid his eyes and started talking faster before he could say anything. "And I don't know if you have been following that whole thing, but I was dating Art Bishop . . ."

Gabe shook his head in confusion. "Wait, what, you were in Kittanning? They are touring right now; my sister just went to their show a few weeks ago. We've had class together all semester." He paused; I could tell he was trying to keep himself from stumbling out more words. Then, slowly, a wave of recognition came over him, and he sat back, hard. "You're Eleanor? The girl that he went on air about and said had run away and gone crazy or something?" He looked at me as if checking for crazy vibes.

He must not have gotten any because he continued, "The song you wrote, was it about him? Was Art Bishop the one who hurt you? Also, isn't the entire music industry looking for you right now?" His face was full of sorrow and empathy mixed with an appropriate dash of confusion.

I shifted uncomfortably. "Yes, and yes, and yes again. And I guess those who believed Art are looking for me." I gave a small smile. "But I have a small rebellion on my side." I had hoped Gabe was the one person who had somehow missed hearing about Art's search party. "But what he said, that isn't what happened at all."

"Okay. Of course, I believe you. Wow, you were in Kittanning. That is a huge deal." I could tell he wasn't sure what he was supposed to say. He scootched closer. "Why are you telling me this now?"

"Because Rebecca Davis knew who I was when you sent her the video of us singing karaoke, and that was why she wanted to come and see our open mic night."

He inhaled sharply. "Oh my gosh, I am *so* sorry if I did something to mess up your disappearance."

"No, actually, the opposite." I told him about my interview with Rebecca, including her article and the morning show interview she had arranged. "I wanted to tell you before she ran the article. You deserve to know the truth, and I wanted you to hear it from me."

"I guess this means you're going to be dropping our class, huh?"

I had to laugh.

"Yeah. I want to see if I can make it as a solo artist without a band. I have never been sure if I could or not. But I guess I also wanted to say thank you." I could feel tears pricking my eyes. "Thank you for believing in me; you helped me find the courage I needed to start over. All my life, I wanted to start a band; I wanted to find my people. You know?" I tried to explain, "People talk about their 'tribe'—the ones they can count on. I've been looking for my 'band'—people who see me and know me and love me for who I am. For a long time, I thought I had that. I had been a member of Kittanning; what more could I have wanted?"

Gabe put his arm around me comfortingly and drew me close as I tried to make it through what I wanted to say. "The other night, even though it was just you and me on the stage, I felt like I was part of something. Like maybe I would get a second chance to belong, to be known and loved."

"Wow. Cynthia starts a band," he said with a laugh.

I looked up at him and smiled wryly. "A.k.a. Eleanor leaves a band."

Gabe wiped a tear off my cheek. "Well, I guess I can check 'share a stage with a celebrity' off my bucket list."

"I hope you don't think I'm crazy. Especially with everything that has been said about me. I don't know what happened; I really didn't mean to run off to just end up going right back to music."

"I don't think someone like you can ever run away from music; I think that it is who you are. I think it will follow you wherever you might go. Some parts of us are just innately who we are. Music is that for you."

He was right, of course. There was no amount of running that would ever let me entirely escape music. It was more than just something I was good at; it was a part of me. I would be rejecting my identity if I turned my back on music.

Gabe was still looking at me intently. I gathered my courage and met his eyes. "I was wondering if you would want to come to the show I am doing. I mean, I know you probably have plans or whatever. I know this is super last minute, and I don't know if what I just told you changes anything. Not that this was anything," I could feel myself blushing and stumbling over my words. "No pressure. I get that you have your own life, and I just really don't want this to change anything between us. Not that there's anything between us. I mean, I'm not against there being something . . ." I was rambling. "Umm, maybe we should go?" I grabbed my bag, embarrassed, and stood up to leave.

"Cynthia. Eleanor." Gabe stood up, gently taking my hand in his. "Are you kidding me? I will be there for you." He grinned softly.

"I mean, if you bring your fiddle, you're welcome to join me on stage," I said with a wink.

"Oh, really?" he said, taking me in his arms. "Can I just say I always knew you were going to be a big star?"

"Mhmm," I said.

And then I kissed him.

24

August 23rd

Eleanor

There was a rush from being on stage that was unlike anything Eleanor had ever felt. Nothing in the world was quite like a crowd surrounding you, cheering for you, rooting for you. The energy and the excitement were incredible.

Yes, she might have been counting down the days until she could have a break, but she had to admit that this was who she was. She would miss it, even if she would only be separated from the stage for a week.

Tonight, they were in Denver. They were covering one of her all-time favorite songs, "Ho, Hey." She really did like the crowd in Denver. There was something special about Colorado.

"Ho, Hey" was near the end of their setlist, two songs before the encore. This was kind of unusual for their cover song; they usually put them near the middle. Art had insisted, and Eleanor did not have the will to fight him. Besides, he had not complained when she had suggested a Lumineers' song. In fact, he was the one who had proposed "Ho, Hey" because he knew it was her favorite.

She decided to pick her battles. She was so close to getting a break from him.

"How are you tonight, Denver!" she yelled into her mic. The crowd started roaring in response. "We like to honor the cities we play by doing something a little special for them. We are proud of where we come from, and we know that you are proud of the artists who have come out of Colorado. Tonight, we honor you by singing what is actually my favorite song, 'Ho, Hey,' by the Lumineers." She was again met with a roar.

They started to sing. Eleanor had the first line. Unbeknownst to her, she had been joined on stage by the Lumineers, who started singing along.

Being on stage is already a surreal experience; there is nothing in the world quite like it. And then, to be suddenly joined by another band you have loved and looked up to is something else. For Eleanor, the next five and a half minutes were some of the most emotional she had ever experienced.

As soon as she heard the familiar voices behind her, she was filled with joy, quickly followed by confusion. What were they doing on the stage? Was she supposed to keep singing? How was this even happening? Who had organized this?

She kept on singing her part. This might be the best show of her life. How had this happened? Her face ached from smiling. This was the best tour surprise ever.

And then, out of nowhere, Art gave her a funny look. The singing stopped. And Art got on one knee, in front of a stadium full of witnesses. And asked her to marry him.

She had to say yes.

Well, actually, she said nothing. She might have made a gesture that looked like a head nod before finding herself wrapped in the arms of Art, who spun her around as if she were a rag doll, and the whole arena went wild around them.

She now understood why this song had been at the end of the setlist. She understood why Art had not fought her when she suggested singing a song from The Lumineers. She knew why one of her favorite bands was on the stage with her. The whole thing had been a setup. The entire thing was staged to make him look like he cared about the things she loved and cared about.

But he didn't care about her enough to wait to hear her answer.

Indeed, Art realized for the first time that she might say no. He saw the look of fear and anger flash over her eyes. Her refusal would, of course, be a significant PR blunder for him. He would have been humiliated. Instead, he embraced a shocked Eleanor and spun her around as if in celebration so that the crowd would think she had said yes.

There had never been a room fuller of joy.

For everyone except one person.

Eleanor had never thought twice about the old saying, "the show must go on," because to her, of course, it must. What reason would someone have to stop a show? People paid to see you perform. You had been practicing this for months. No matter what was going on in your personal life, this was your job. You had to be able to set it aside for two hours. The show must go on.

She had never thought twice about this expression until she found herself being swung around the stage. She hadn't practiced this part. She had no idea what she was supposed to do now.

If this had happened anywhere other than on her stage, she would have said no. She would have run away. But Art had asked her to marry him in the one place where he knew that she could not refuse.

He had set the whole thing up flawlessly. Eleanor had to at least give credit where credit was due.

So, the show went on. Eleanor made a vague remark about her joyful surprise in sharing this moment with her fans. The same fans who had walked with her and Art through their whole relationship. They cheered.

And the lights went out. The show was over.

And she ran.

Art would tell people that he had talked with Eleanor after the show: she had been gushing about how excited and happy she was about the engagement. He lied. His path hadn't crossed Eleanor's once they left the post-show area.

Jenny thought Eleanor was on the phone with someone backstage, so she didn't stop to talk to her. Instead, Jenny had done a dance in celebration as she walked past. Jenny had assumed that Eleanor was calling her family, who had, oddly enough, not been in the crowd that night. Really, the engagement was a good move. The more Jenny had talked to Art, the more he had convinced her of his love for Eleanor. Jenny couldn't help but root for love.

Chip thought he saw Eleanor rushing to her dressing room after the show, but he had figured that she was just changing quickly before joining them for their post-show drink.

James hadn't seen Eleanor after the show. She had seen him but had avoided him at all costs. She didn't know if she was more mad or disappointed or scared of his reaction. Had James known? Or worse, had he approved? James, if he were honest with himself, wasn't sure what he thought either. But there was no denying that this would be the best headlining story in the band's history. That had to count for something.

No one had seen Eleanor leave the arena. It was not until they discovered her empty dressing room with Art's grandmother's ring shining dimly on her dresser that they realized what had happened.

Eleanor Quinn was gone.

Cora had always known that the Eleanor she had grown up with would never date a guy like Art. Cora knew that Eleanor had never gotten along with him. Her parents talked about the tense relationship all the time. They felt sorry for their poor, famous daughter—as if having a bad coworker was something no one else had suffered through.

Except, deep down, Cora knew Art was different. He was toxic and manipulative. When she had dated him, he would read her text messages, micro-manage her life, make her feel like nothing, and then make her beg for a scrap of his attention. How could her sister have actually gone out with someone like him? This had to be some sort of mistake.

Seeing them in a relationship felt like a profound betrayal.

Then, there was the over-the-top engagement. People she hadn't talked to in years called Cora to tell her how happy they were for her sister. In fact, that was how she found out her sister was engaged. A high school classmate who now worked in Denver had been at that concert and had seen it and called Cora right away, thinking that Cora might be at the show.

Cora had been shocked.

But her parents had been shocked, too. They were also in Pennsylvania instead of in Denver for the engagement.

That was when she knew something was up. She messaged Eleanor's friend, Jess, to see if she knew anything. But Jess hadn't heard anything from Eleanor since before the engagement. She seemed really worried.

In a move of pure desperation, Cora did what she had sworn to never do—she called Art. She regretted it the moment he picked up the phone. But it confirmed what she had suspected: Eleanor had made a break for it. This was the Eleanor she had grown up with. She almost felt a little proud of her sister's radio silent disappearance.

November 3rd

Cynthia/Eleanor

Eleanor Quinn, I have to say, I am amazed and honored to be talking with you this morning!" The news anchor greeted me warmly. We had strategically chosen for the interview to be done on *Wake Up, America* because it was the rival show of the one where Art had given his interview. I was in Rebecca's office because it looked more professional than Kristy's apartment. We had carefully selected my outfit and my surroundings to make it clear I was not crazy.

"Thank you so much for having me. I wish I could be with you in New York, but I am actually playing a show in Seattle tomorrow night, and I wanted to stay here to prepare."

"I didn't know what to think when my producer originally pitched this story, but really, it is an honor to get to talk with you today." She turned to her audience. "If you haven't seen already, the *Seattle Times* ran a story yesterday detailing Eleanor's side of the story and her departure from the band Kittanning. I am sure many people have heard or seen reports from Art Bishop, your former bandmate, proclaiming that you had gone crazy and run away from the band. Eleanor, what made you want to tell your side of the story?"

"I wanted to tell my story because I was tired of feeling voiceless. I remember watching Art's interview and thinking that my life was over. In one interview, it felt like he killed my career and hard-earned reputation. But everything he said was a lie. As I said in the article, the relationship between Art and myself was fabricated by Kittanning's record label. Most of the fabrication was done by our manager, James Porzio. It was correctly calculated that we, as a couple, would boost the band's likability. Neither Art nor I were given a choice; we simply had to go along with it. I felt trapped, and I felt like I had lost my voice."

"In the article, you talk about your relationship with Art, before and after the 'couple' set up. Tell me more about that."

"Yes, the whole relationship was a fabrication. I have evidence to prove this; I was trying to get out of it as quickly as possible. Art and I had never been friends. We had always been cordial, though it was common knowledge around the industry that we didn't get along. He saw this relationship as a way to improve his reputation. But throughout our time of fake dating, Art was verbally abusive and manipulative and even attempted physical abuse. For me, it was a toxic situation that felt hopeless. It wasn't a normal relationship, and I wasn't allowed to break up with him. There was no way for me to get out. I didn't want to end things and risk my career, which I had worked my whole life to develop."

"I am so sorry to hear that you were put through a situation like that. I cannot imagine how that must have felt. What was the tipping point for you?"

"Like I said, I felt voiceless and powerless, but I knew that I needed to do something. I had been planning to leave if James or the label didn't 'allow' us to break up. He and Art both threatened me separately about what speaking out would do to my career. It was petrifying, a situation that I would never wish upon anyone. But then, the night of the proposal put everything in perspective. I felt shocked and blindsided, and suddenly, I knew that for the people calling the shots on my life, the relationship between Art and me had no end in sight. I didn't really think about what I was doing. I just got on a bus and headed to Seattle."

"Why Seattle?"

"I have a cousin who lives here, and I knew that I needed to go somewhere safe but not obvious."

"Okay, so now I have to ask you the question that America has been dying to know. What have you been doing the past three months?"

"I wanted to start over. At first, I wasn't sure what that meant, but I knew that I needed, for my own health, to leave Kittanning as far behind as possible. I mourned and grieved that loss before I realized that I needed to do something, or I was going to drive myself crazy. One of my favorite things about being in a band was the songwriting I got to do, so I decided to enroll in an English class. I didn't learn much other than I am a much better songwriter than I am a novelist."

"I know that your music and lyrics have touched the hearts of many. You mentioned that you have a concert tomorrow night. Does that mean that we can expect to see you back in the music world?"

"I have learned a lot in these past few months about myself. This was really the first time since I was sixteen that I have had the power to make my own choices. I moved to Seattle to start fresh. I thought that I could have a clean break from my old life and start over, no questions asked. But what I learned in this process is that some things follow you no matter what. It's as if they are a core piece of who you are. For me, that's music. I couldn't escape being a musician. I think no matter where in the world I am, no matter how hard I try to run away from it, music will always be a major part of who I am. So, without me looking for it, music found me again. I have been writing, and I am hoping to start recording soon as a solo artist."

"Wow, I am sure that your fans are celebrating today, not only because there is the hope of new music but because you are safe. If people want to see your show tomorrow, how can they do that?"

"The tickets are free. I mostly just want people to show up. Any donations will be donated to a local non-profit helping women get out of violent situations. I have been writing new songs, and I am really excited to share them with the world. This might be the most nervous for a show I have ever been." The last sentence wasn't an exaggeration; my palms were also the sweatiest they had ever been.

"I had the honor of hearing one of the songs you wrote, and it was my favorite song you have ever written. It is so powerful, and I think you put into words the story of what you walked through in a way that will relate to so many. I think this song will really have an effect on a lot of people."

"Thank you. The song is called, 'Wasn't Love,' and tomorrow morning, I will be releasing it as a single. I met a few people here in Seattle who helped me record it. I am really excited to get my music out into the world."

"Eleanor, it has been my privilege to talk with you this morning, and I am so excited to hear about what comes next."

"Thank you!" I said. As soon as the screen went blank, I let out a sigh I didn't realize I had been holding in.

I was getting to share my story.

Time felt as if it were moving at double speed. My parents and brother were arriving tonight so that they could be there to support me tomorrow. This had been the longest I had gone without seeing them. I was bursting with excitement.

I didn't know how it would feel doing a show the same weekend as Kittanning. They had no way to contact me, which was relieving.

It had gotten out that Jess was staying with Kristy and me. At this point, we had all moved into a hotel so we could have better security protection. Jenny had reached out to Jess. Her text was simple, which in some ways felt more sincere, "Tell Eleanor I am sorry and that I believe her. If there is a ticket, I would love to come to her show."

I loved Jenny.

James and Art had both called Jess multiple times. She blocked their numbers.

Gabe had asked if I wanted to go to Kittanning's show, just to see if they addressed my interview. I didn't think there would ever be a day where I could watch Art on stage without feeling sick to my stomach.

Instead, that night, I was trying to distract myself by going over the songs I would be playing one more time.

Jess burst into the room. "You are not going to believe what happened."

"What?"

"Jenny and Chip walked off the stage."

"Wait, what!" This felt impossible.

"Jenny took the mic and said that she stands in solidarity with you. She basically admitted to standing by and doing nothing when she suspected something bad was happening. She said she naïvely let herself believe you were okay, and she should have done something sooner. They had only sung like two songs before they walked off. They were supposed to sing 'Home,' and as she was doing the drum intro for it, she stopped, said her piece, and then she and Chip just walked off the stage."

"You are kidding me! What did the crowd do—what did Art do? Did anyone release a statement?"

"So, I guess the crowd was already smaller than expected. Most people boycotted. The people who did go were mostly there to hear what the band was going to say. But from the video I saw, most people cheered when they walked off. Kittanning hasn't posted an official statement yet. I think Art did a shortened set by himself."

"I seriously can't believe that happened. I guess Art finally gets to live out his dream of not having to share the stage. What a way to kickstart your solo career."

"Is it terrible that I can't stop thinking about how amazing this is?" Jess asked.

"Are you kidding me? This might actually be the highlight of my career."

I couldn't wrap my head around Jenny walking off the stage for me. She had walked away in a move that could end her career.

I felt an overwhelming urge to cry. She was willing to sacrifice everything that she had worked for to validate my story.

"Can I use your phone?"

Jess handed it over wordlessly and left to swim laps at the hotel pool.

I called Jenny. She answered on the second ring.

"Is this Eleanor, Cynthia, or Jess?" she joked as soon as she answered.

"Jenny," I tried to think of something to say next, but I was suddenly speechless. "I cannot believe that you would do that for me. Thank you."

"I believe you. As soon as I read your story, I knew it was all true. I have worked with Art long enough to know how he acts. I am just really so sorry that I didn't do anything sooner," she sobbed. "I am so sorry."

"I forgive you. Also, what are you doing tomorrow night? Do you want to come drum for me?"

"Well, seeing as it looks like I am no longer employed, I would love that."

"I'll send you the information." I paused. "I don't know what to do to thank you."

"Remember me when you're famous." I could hear her smile through the phone.

I was left alone to celebrate this victory for maybe twenty minutes before Kristy knocked on our shared door.

"Hey, E, your sister is here. Can she talk with you?"

I hadn't seen or heard from Cora in over a year. I honestly couldn't remember the last time the two of us had a conversation without our parents present.

"Um, yeah, of course."

"Hey," Cora said almost shyly. That was a change; Cora had never been shy. "Can I come in?"

"Yeah, of course." I stared at her swaying awkwardly, hands in her pockets, as if she didn't know if she should stand or sit. I was not going to be the one to start this conversation.

"Hey, so I got here as quickly as I could, and I wasn't sure if you would even want to talk to me or anything, but I guess I just needed to hear it from you. Was it true? I mean, what you said in the interview and in the article?"

"Yes, every word." And then I remembered, a little too late, that Cora had dated Art in high school. By her own choice, not by force. "Wait, Cora, was he like this when you were going out with him?"

"Yes, I thought that you knew. That was why I couldn't be around you after the band started. I felt so betrayed. I always thought you knew what he was like and chose to just ignore it. When I saw that you guys were dating, or, I guess, 'dating,'"— Cora made air quotes with her fingers—"I thought maybe he had changed. But when he did that interview and said that you had gone crazy, I don't know. I guess I just knew something was off."

I didn't know what to say.

"Did you know I was in Seattle?"

"Yeah, mom told me, but I didn't think you would want to see me, and I wasn't even sure what to say. I guess I should have said sorry and that I should have warned you. I was so young, I guess a part of me just thought love was like that. And you were going to be a rock star, and I felt so covered in shame. I didn't want you to think differently of me, and I didn't want to ruin the band."

We sat in silence for a long time. I felt righteously angry. How had this happened? How had I let this happen?

"How long are you in Seattle? Will you come to my show tomorrow night?"

Tears welled in her eyes. "Yes."

I don't think there will ever be a place where I feel more at home than on the stage. There is something about it that just feels natural.

Tonight would be no exception.

Jenny had, in fact, joined me as my drummer. Jess sang two songs as an opener for me. We had always said it would be a dream to play the same stage.

Randy was leading the security team. Under no circumstances would James or Art be allowed into the building. In theory, they should be on their way to their next show by now, but Kittanning's drummer was currently on my stage, and their lead guitar player was in the wings cheering us on. I doubted the tour would go on as scheduled.

Reuniting with Jenny felt awkward but natural at the same time. As soon as she saw me, she apologized profusely. She told me that, as soon as my article was published, she and Chip decided to stage a walk-off. She said that knowing the truth, there was no way she could continue with the rest of the tour and live with herself.

So, they walked. Jenny told me that James had been calling her all day. She had ignored every one of his calls. Chip had agreed to deal with him.

This show felt like a strange mixture of intimacy and vulnerability. A smaller local record label that Rebecca knew and trusted had released "Wasn't Love" for us. It had debuted this morning. There was no way to take it back now. Which felt almost as freeing as that night I left Kittanning.

"I'm not sure if you know this, but I used to sing in a little band called Kittanning," I addressed the crowd as I walked onto the stage. "I don't know if you're here because you're a fan of Kittanning, and you wanted to see the girl who went crazy, or if you are a fan of me, or if you just had nothing better to do on a Saturday night. Either way, I am glad you're here."

This was my first time addressing a crowd on my own; there was no one to banter back and forth with. I looked to my right, where I could see Gabe standing in the wings, beaming at me.

"I wanted to open with a song that might be the most personal song I have ever written. As most of you know, I was forced to be in a relationship with Art Bishop. I spent those months justifying and writing off the way that he treated me. This next song is for all of the women who have ever justified abusive behaviors for the sake of what they think is love."

I could tell my voice was about to crack through my suppressed tears. This song felt different performing live to a group of people who understood more of the lyrics' backstory. I took a deep breath and glanced around me, sustained by the smiling faces of the people I love. Even though I was alone on the stage, I felt more like a member of a band than I ever had. Kristy, Jenny, Gabe, Chip, Randy, and Cora were the band I had been searching for my entire life.

Finally, the first words came out of my mouth.

I thought it was my fault
That we didn't work
I blamed myself
I took on that hurt
I didn't tell anyone, those things you said to me
I thought it was love, isn't this how it's supposed to be?

But I've spoken up now
I've found my voice

That wasn't love
That wasn't love
That wasn't love
No, it wasn't love
When you told me you loved me
You didn't mean it
You didn't mean it
And when everything fell apart you said it was me
You told me not to tell those things you had done
Because you had a future and I had none
But I'm done keeping your secrets
For the sake of love

I didn't think they would believe me
If I told the truth
Because I convinced the world I meant it
When I said I loved you
And I kept quiet
Out of fear

But I'm done living that way
Now I am singing it loud for the world to hear

That wasn't love
That wasn't love
That wasn't love
No, it wasn't love
When you told me you loved me
You didn't mean it
You didn't mean it
And when everything fell apart you said it was me
You told me not to tell those things you had done
Because you had a future and I had none
But I'm done keeping your secrets
For the sake of love
You told the world I'd gone crazy
And that was what was making me tell all those lies
You told my best friend you didn't need me, all my drama
That was why you were glad to tell me goodbye
So go on and tell your friends that I am some kind of liar
Tell them I'm pathetic
But you and I will always know the truth of that night
We know
That wasn't love
That wasn't love
That wasn't love
No, it wasn't love
When you told me you loved me
You didn't mean it
You didn't mean it

And when everything fell apart you said it was me
You told me not to tell those things you had done
Because you had a future and I had none
But I'm done keeping your secrets
For the sake of love.

Everything suddenly felt like it was falling into place. As soon as I sang the last note, the lights went up, and the crowd went wild.

And that is how Eleanor Quinn left a band, and Cynthia started one.

About the Author

Olivia Swindler was raised in Spokane, Washington but currently resides in Grenoble, France, where she consumes approximately a baguette a day. She serves as the Communication Coordinator for Young Life in Europe. *Cynthia Starts a Band* is her first book.

A free ebook edition is available with the purchase of this book.

To claim your free ebook edition:

1. Visit MorganJamesBOGO.com
2. Sign your name CLEARLY in the space
3. Complete the form and submit a photo of the entire copyright page
4. You or your friend can download the ebook to your preferred device

Morgan James
BOGO™

A **FREE** ebook edition is available for you or a friend with the purchase of this print book.

CLEARLY SIGN YOUR NAME ABOVE

Instructions to claim your free ebook edition:
1. Visit MorganJamesBOGO.com
2. Sign your name CLEARLY in the space above
3. Complete the form and submit a photo of this entire page
4. You or your friend can download the ebook to your preferred device

Print & Digital Together Forever.

Snap a photo

Free ebook

Read anywhere